LITTLE BLUE MARBLE 2021

TIPPING POINTS

EDITED BY KATRINA ARCHER

A Ganache Media Book

Vancouver

2021 Ganache Media Print edition

Cover design by Katrina Archer

www.ganachemedia.com

littlebluemarble.ca

LITTLE BLUE MARBLE
2021
TIPPING POINTS

For all of those determined to be on the right side of history

CONTENTS

INTRODUCTION

WELCOME to the collected stories and poems of *Little Blue Marble* from 2021. All of these stories are available for free online because *Little Blue Marble*'s mission is to educate and inspire, not to make a profit. We thank you, however, because your purchase of this anthology will help us bring the world more great stories about the climate crisis, and keep our mission on track.

2021 brought us several events that make it hard to deny we are hurtling towards climate tipping points. The town of Lytton, BC, north of 50° latitude, broke the Canadian heat record three times in one week, topping out at 49.6°C—a temperature hotter than the hottest ever in Las Vegas, far to the south. The day after smashing this high, Lytton burned to the ground in a devastating wildfire. The heat dome that brought about these temperatures marched across the continent, causing massive crop failures and over 500 deaths in the province of British Columbia alone.

The drought in the American Southwest is now the worst in recorded history, causing water levels to drop alarmingly in the region's watersheds, and exacerbating a historic wildfire season that has reduced air quality for weeks and months at a time in large portions of western American states and Canadian provinces to dangerous levels, affecting the health of millions.

Flash flooding in a dozen countries in Europe killed approximately 250 people. The flooding has been tied to the increasing likelihood of severe weather events caused by the climate crisis.

As our leaders fiddle with half measures, or actively block meaningful legislation because of their own ties to the fossil fuel industry, it becomes more and more clear that the changes we have effected to the planet run the risk of becoming irreversible.

Here's to stepping back from the brink before it's too late.

— *Katrina Archer, Publisher & Editor*, Little Blue Marble

EXILED TOGETHER: FACES OF CONTEMPORARY NEW YORK

Marcus M. Tyler

FROM *Exiled Together: Faces of Contemporary New York*, Online Edition:

• • •

"My grandfather was a Navy man. He sailed all over the world, the Bay of Bengal, the Pacific Islands. Wherever he went, he had the same mission: keep the peace. Also shore up our influence in the seas, but we don't need to get into that. What matters is he kept a diary. Every place he went he wrote down conversations with locals, what they wore, what they ate. He did this because he knew these places were more fragile than dreams, because someday they would all be gone, all these unique people with their unique ways of being. Even New York would someday face the same fate, he said. When he got home he uploaded a copy of his diary to the Library of Congress. He told me it was the most important thing he has ever done."

—*Julian, 1 August 2117*

• • •

"Oh God, what's happened? Oh God, oh, how could this happen to our city? I'm heartbroken. Sorry, but I don't think I can talk to you right now."

—*Xinyi, 6 October 2117*

• • •

"My family moved here from the Philippines during the Second Wave. I was a little girl then and don't remember much about the islands, except the palm trees. We don't have those in Brooklyn. All that's to say my home is here, and I don't know what I'll do if we have to leave. We've had no power for three weeks. We've had no tap water. Can't say how many hours I've lost on hold with the city. They say they're sorting it out. They keep filing tickets and never do anything. You know, I have a friend in Staten Island who got through in fifteen minutes, and they sent someone over the next day. Only difference I can see is my family lives in the immigrant blocks."

—*Mayumi, 25 October 2117*

• • •

"We traveled to the Venetian ruins, my honey and me, back in our first year dating. She was the sweetest darling in the world, always full of grand ideas. We spent many a night whispering by the fireside, with what few cold nights we get here in Queens. Oh, she was just a darling. But you were asking about Venice, right? When we went, she told me something that changed my life. She said she'd always wanted to get married by that campanile, the one that juts from the sea like some sunken Egyptian monolith. We'd never even talked about marriage before, but we got married on the spot, on the gondola, with the oarsman as our witness. It's like it created some unbreakable bond between us and that place. Strange how we came home and the water came with us."

—*Sasha, 2 November 2117*

• • •

"When the water came I didn't even know anything was wrong. Not at first. I picked up my daughter from school, and she had this curious look like she'd seen something that didn't make sense. But she didn't say anything, so we kept walking. She was nine and I'd been trying to give her more independence. Well, we got home to Harlem and she turned to me with big eyes. And she said, 'Papa, why are we supposed to stay out of the subways today?' I just froze."

—*Marlin, 3 November 2117*

• • •

"I was on the first response team when the levee broke, and believe me when I tell you it was not something I'm keen on reliving. No, I'm not upset at you asking, it's just that it changes a man. I still dream about it. All the people I could not save come visit me at night, face after nameless face. My neighbour's daughter is one of them. He called me first thing when the rumours broke online, and it took me two days to get enough reception to call him back. When I finally told him what happened he cried right there on the phone. Broke my heart like all the other deaths could not."

—*Darrin, 13 November 2117*

• • •

"They're saying now the Siberians blew out the Hudson Levee, with a supersonic underwater munition or what. I don't believe the lot of them. I was in my apartment on 90th and didn't see nothing. No, I don't want to elaborate. I was in my apartment, like I told you. I didn't see or hear nothing. The seawater's not the problem. The only problem's us overreacting over nothing. And that's just how the Siberians want it."

—*Anonymous, 15 November 2117*

• • •

"When I was a girl I remember sitting on my great-grandma's lap, and hearing her tell me all these incredible stories about the world before the Warming. You'd think I would cry for the people we've lost, the migrations and famines. But let me tell you, I lived through the New York thing, and still it's the frogs I think about at night. My great-grandma loved the frogs. They came in all colours, blues and bright yellows, green ones with red eyes. I've seen pictures too, but it's not much more than I could do with a computer and a pair of hands. I mean, I've seen deepfakes that look more real. But those frogs really came in all colours. It's the colours that mark the evolution of the world, you know. Now all we have are pale greens and greys, bone-white skies. There used to be flowers and bees, too, outside the greenhouses. There was once a time when all the colours of our world were taken for granted, and now they're gone, and I cry that we will never get them back."

—*Yvonne, 16 December 2117*

• • •

"As a public elementary teacher I'm often asked, 'How do you teach young children about the Warming? How can you stand before them and explain that a world was lost, and we could have done something about it but we did not?' Well, it's really not so hard. These people, see, they look at me with this emptiness in their eyes, like life is a joyless toil with no purpose. But that's not what I see when I look at the kids. The kids haven't yet learned how to despair. Sure, there's sadness in their eyes, sometimes, and fear, especially after what happened in October. But there's life and laughter in them too, mischief and curiosity, and optimism. They really come from all walks of life. So when I tell them about the mass extinctions, and the global migrations, they're actually much more mature talking about these things than many of the adults I know. Do I know what will happen in the aftermath of October's attack? No, and I told them so, and that answer was good enough for them. I tell them, as long as the people of New York stand, as long as you take care of your community, the rest of the world stands a chance too.

The sheer diversity of New York is a testament to our resilience against all we've lost, and I'll stand by that to the end."

—*Bao, 21 December 2117*

ABOUT THE AUTHOR

Marcus M. Tyler is a science fiction and fantasy writer living in Austin, Texas. He especially likes to write stories with immersive settings, and stories that give the reader a sense of culture shock, whether that be in a historical period on Earth or an entirely fictional universe. He is also a technical writer and does research in artificial intelligence, where he explores how to use data in ethical and equitable ways. In his free time he plays guitar and enjoys a good cappuccino. Find him on Twitter @MarcusMTyler.

THE MONTH THAT THE RAINS CAME

John F. McMullen

JULY 2021
It seems to me
that there has
been more rain
than any time
in memory

But that was
only in the
US Northeast

In the Pacific
Northwest and
western Canada

hundreds die
from the heat

An entire small
Canadian town
is destroyed from
the heat and the
"Bootleg Fire"
in Northern
Oregon covers
more space than
New York City

Covid19 spikes
in Mississippi and
Missouri after
already killing
more than half a
million in the US

Outside the US
hundreds in
Germany and
Belgium are
killed by
flash floods

In this battle
of insults
when Nature
says *Fuck You*
to us it does
no good for us
to say

       so's your mother ... Or

       wanna make something of it?

or to send in the Marines
we need another answer and soon

ABOUT THE AUTHOR

John F. McMullen, *"johnmac the bard"*, is an adjunct professor
at Westchester Community College, a graduate of Iona
College, the holder of two Masters degrees from Marist
College, a member of the American Academy of Poets and
Poets & Writers, the author of over 2,500 columns and ten
books (*eight poetry, the most recent of which is* My Life In 26
Poems *(2021)*), and a contributor to many anthologies.
Additionally, he has been the host of a weekly Internet Radio
Show (*three hundred shows to date*) and hosted many Zoom
poetry and writers meetings throughout the pandemic.

SWEETEN THE DEAL

Dan Micklethwaite

HER first days in the city, Jeanette had been jealous of Rhodri's tomatoes and Michaela's zucchinis with their shiny green skin. Also of Angelo's chillies and lemongrass. And Dominic's flourishing plot of begonias—in spite of the fact they weren't really allowed; the block's rooftop biodome was for edibles only.

Still, she would have gladly grown flowers as well. She would have grown anything. She *had* to grow something, to cover her rent. But with all of the packing and stress of the move, she had forgotten to bring any seeds.

As her neighbours all worked underneath the dome's ceiling—with its solar panels and rain pipes that cast shadows like clouds—and she breathed the warm, filtered air with its absence of wind, she felt useless and lonely as never before. In their labour-stained overalls and with caps and bandanas, they resembled propaganda from a previous age.

We can do it!
We're all in this together!
Except no one looked back, let alone offered help.

• • •

She had come here to meet people and attend university, to make more of herself and get on in the world. But she only got homesick. And when her folks sent a package, it just made matters worse.

The intercom buzzed to her room to alert her, but when she reached the ground floor, the courier had just left the crate and moved on. Her parents had told her to tip where she could, as gig workers really weren't very well paid, but she was secretly glad that she'd missed the chance now— surviving the month would be tough as it was.

Then guilt washed over her, as she studied the package— it had FRAGILE and CAUTION marked on the side, in her mother's distinctive acrylic swirls, and couldn't have been the easiest item to ship. If she could afford to send anything back to them soon, she would ask for it likewise to be mailed through that courier, and insist upon paying a double tip then.

Though, that was a big if.

It was a big box, and as she wrapped her arms around it and edged towards the elevator, she'd have preferred that she was being hugged instead. That her folks could be with her to soothe all these worries, to finish the discussion they had all three been having, on and off, in the days just before she'd departed their ranch. And yet, the very notion reminded her how tough that would be, with them being among the few still living rural, only sparingly linked to the digital grid.

The elevator was descending from the rooftop again, and she tried hard not to burst into tears while she waited. With a ping, the doors opened, but as she was about to barge in with her package, Mr Kielty, the tenement landlord, appeared. He was a tall, rangy man, balding on top, though with spiky blond eyebrows like ripe ears of wheat. They had helped him seem open and kind on first meeting, but arched ominously now. He scanned Jeanette's face, then the crate, then back up.

"I hope 'FRAGILE' means something is growing in there," he said, without giving so much as a smile for a greeting.

"Erm, I—"

"It's just, there's only three weeks until rent will be due, and I can't help but notice your plot is still bare. Unless you've sown something that ain't sprouted yet? I'm sure you could borrow some compost, if needed."

"Well, I haven't quite—"

"I know it must be a change, coming out from the country, but unlike in the country, things don't grow on trees. Not 'less you're willing to tend them yourself. And with space at a premium, we can't really tolerate freeloaders here."

Jeanette's tear ducts prickled.

"I don't mean to be harsh," Kielty added, "but this was all clear in the contract you signed. In your response and your interview, you told me you'd cope. Told me you'd contribute. And there was a lot of competition for your room and your plot. I don't want to have to relet it so soon, so I hope you'll be able to turn things around. And ask for help if you need it. We're all in this together."

He seemed about to reach out and pat Jeanette's shoulder, except the crate was in the way, and so he simply stepped around her and walked out instead. When the doors closed behind her, she finally sobbed.

• • •

She stared at the package for what felt like hours, tracing her fingertip over the words. FRAGILE. CAUTION. As if her mother had known they'd apply to her life, or at least her current state of mind. In a moment of rebellion, given her parents both frowned on tattoos, she toyed with getting those labels inked on her skin. But pushing her family away would not stop her missing them. She'd probably just miss them more.

Though, that would be hard.

She couldn't wait any longer, tore open the crate. Straightaway some of her resolve came back. For a start, the box was amply padded with straw, which might be useful to others, if not here then at least in some neighbouring blocks, those which held chickens and perhaps even goats. If she had to, she could trade it for peoples' spare crops, to pass off as her own till she could plant something good.

Her resolve only grew when she found the enclosed letter, which smelt not just of hay but of blossom as well. Her parents were embarrassingly old-fashioned at times, or rather a bit too self-consciously *retro*, but the note had a personal, tangible quality, which almost made up for the lack of a hug. They'd doubtless prefer a response in that medium, but Jeannette lacked the patience for writing with pens, and anyway paper was heavily taxed. *Perhaps next month.* She sent them a video "Thank you!" instead—though she didn't know when they'd receive and reply.

Regardless, she'd record them another one later, just as soon as she'd set up their gift.

• • •

There was no sign of the landlord when she got to the elevator, and no one else either, for which she was glad, although moving the crate by herself was hard work. Again, none of her neighbours ventured to help as she awkwardly hefted it onto the roof. And though Mr Kielty had told her to ask them, Jeanette was afraid they'd ignore her request.

We're all in this together.

And yet she still didn't feel she was part of that *we*.

Not at the moment. But hopefully soon.

She found a spare dolly and trundled the crate to her plot at the edge of the roof, where she set about bringing its contents to light. Another box, although not simply recycled plywood this time, but carved and varnished timber from her parents' best stock. Her father had graced it with carvings of flowers—orchids, azaleas—though their message made clear that such things weren't inside. She removed the front panel, trembling slightly, to finally get a good look at what was.

It took them a minute or two to start showing, and while waiting she checked on her neighbours again. With the heat of the day, magnified through the ceiling, they had stripped down to T-shirts and blouses and vests, the sleeves of their overalls tied round their waists. Michaela and Dominic still wore bandanas, and Angelo was in a baseball cap that he removed for a second to wipe sweat from his brow. He seemed about her age or maybe just older, and would likely know where there was nightlife, if any. That had been key to her to move to the city, the desire to experience what she'd only known so far from vids. Not that she'd told that to her parents, of course, or was planning to update them on all her activities.

She would show them the roof, though, and what occurred in her plot. Starting with catching this moment on film. The first sets of tiny antennae emerging, then the heads and front legs and the glimmer of wings, which twitched but were still not quite ready to fly. They seemed a bit pallid, even through a lens filter, and their markings were fuzzy, but the note had assured her the brightness would come. Yellow and black, which could sometimes mean caution, but in this case, the note said, those colours meant life.

The bees would bring honey, and that would pay rent. They would also help crops that had not yet been modded, or otherwise counted on wind pollination, like Rhodri's tomatoes and Michaela's zucchinis. They would keep the begonias blooming as well.

As if they could sense this, her neighbours glanced over. When the buzzing first started, a few of them smiled.

ABOUT THE AUTHOR

Dan Micklethwaite writes stories in a shed in the north of England, some of which have featured in *Daily Science Fiction*, Owl Hollow Press's *When the World Stopped* anthology, and *PodCastle*. His debut novel, *The Less Than Perfect Legend of Donna Creosote*, was published in the UK by Bluemoose Books.

THREE LITTLE ARCOLOGIES

Marie Vibbert

ONCE Upon A Time, there were three little buildings that dreamed of being self-sustaining. One was covered in stone, one in vinyl siding, but the third little building was covered in discarded things, in tar paper and tin foil and whatever happened to be on hand, and it was the strongest of them all.

• • •

The Monmouth building was built in 1932 as a nine-unit apartment building on East 116th Street near then-fashionable Luke Easter Park. Deborah Harris bought the faux-gothic pile in an outrageous bargain that was also an outrageous fortune, and she bragged about it both ways.

Being a landlady was in her blood. Her mother, Elena Harris, had owned two up-down duplexes in East Cleveland. One had been her grandmother's home but by the time

Deborah was born they only visited to sign leases or deliver eviction notices.

Her grandmother's neighbourhood starved and withered from never enough money or never enough time, and the grand houses sagged with decay. Deborah vowed to make something that could feed itself, that could withstand all the privations mankind could manufacture.

The first thing she did with her small business loan was replace Monmouth's aging roof with molded "slate" solar panels. She cleared the dumbwaiter shaft—which had sat unused save for the ground floor, where it held snow shovels—to create a water filtration tower. She provided the large balconies, soaked in sunlight, with plant beds.

With her vision and careful planning, Deborah harnessed water and sun and soil. All she needed were some tenants to live in her sustainable house made of stone and hope.

• • •

Meanwhile, the Big Bad Development Company gobbled up buildings all over Ohio, tearing them down to build luxury condominiums that looked pretty on the outside but were all particle board and aluminum struts on the inside, designed to fall down within ten years so people would be forced to buy another one.

• • •

Thi Pham wasn't looking to buy a big house, but a coworker was having trouble unloading her place out in North Royalton, and the deal was too good to pass up. It was a nondescript McMansion in a neighbourhood of McMansions, but this one had been cut into four rental units. The centre unit, containing the grand foyer and living room, was more than enough space for Thi and her plants, and the income from the rental units would help pay the mortgage.

The foyer had an enormous skylight, making the shaft-like room almost a greenhouse. The stairs ended at a blank wall now that the second floor had been made into its own apartment. Thi would festoon the steps with plants, and they would grow until tendrils hung like a waterfall over the ostentatious faux-marble panelling.

Thi had studied forestry and botany in college, but she worked with government agencies, helping new immigrants settle in Cleveland, so she heard about every new program. She applied for a grant to turn the two-storey wall in her foyer into a green wall.

Then her first month's rent money vanished into her tenants' electric bill.

Thi used part of the green-wall money to install a wind turbine to take some of the load off. She would have a few months of cash-strapped struggle, but if she kept nurturing it, soon her big house of vinyl and ambition would be running itself.

• • •

Big Bad Development Company stalked the suburbs, sniffing out homeowners' associations and business-minded local politicians that could help it ravage properties. Sleepy, affluent suburbs eagerly welcomed the Big Bad Company and rushed to shower it in affection and new zoning regulations.

• • •

Gentle Rain Higgins was born into the Hessler House cooperative, though she'd left to pursue a business degree that got her called "sellout" for years. Being house manager was always more work and less gratitude, but the photos in the front lobby of cops dragging people out of the building served as a constant reminder of a noble past, and what happened when you broke housing codes.

Hessler House had been a privately owned cooperative since the Sixties, cobbled together between two houses that had been cut into apartments and then joined together. Some walls were pressboard, some fibreboard, some straw. Some you didn't want to think about too closely, but they were all in good repair. There was a waiting list to move in, and few ever left once they settled, so Gentle had to do some creative thinking to make room while staying up to code.

Hessler was nothing if not creative. The grey water system began in the Eighties, using rain to supplement the toilets. When the city couldn't ban the collector as an eyesore, they up and banned rain barrels of all kinds. That was OK. The fire escape on the back of the building, well, it suddenly had new, fat columns made of PVC. Funny, that. You had to climb on the roof to see the gutter lines, hand-painted brown with woodgrain-mimicking swirls, feeding into the columns. Invisible from the ground. During storms, however, you could hear the musical waterfalls inside.

Hessler House was as organic as the tomatoes grown in the window boxes, and Gentle never saw herself living anywhere other than this house made of brick, straw, wood, garbage, and solidarity.

• • •

The three little arcologies prospered. Deborah's stone Monmouth filled with residents, especially the front "garden" units. Deborah's books were balanced and her water recycler tower worked a charm.

Thi was so impressed with the success of her windmill that she added a leach field and organic wastewater recycling to her vinyl McMansion. Her cash flow would be precarious, but projected to improve.

To alleviate the waiting list, Hessler House acquired the house next door. Finances would be tight, but they had a strong volunteer group to renovate the place. The first symbolic connection was an arbour over the alley between them. With the neighbour's cars gone, the alley became the new home of the chicken coop. The residents strung lights overhead and played music to celebrate on a warm summer night.

• • •

Big Bad Development scanned the area for new houses to gobble up. It saw the three little arcologies, and liked what it saw.

First it approached the house made of stone.

• • •

"You can't revoke the permit—the work's been done!" Deborah had taken the whole day and been routed through a half-dozen offices before arriving at the zoning commission responsible for shutting down her water recycling project.

"The sustainable building act only covers *new* construction," the tired woman behind the desk said. "I'm sorry, but what we're encouraging others to do is illegal for you."

"Why in heaven's name is it illegal? Is it safety? Materials? I have reports—"

"I don't make the rules." She gestured helplessly over the mess on her desk.

Deborah recognized herself in this woman, and pulled her frustration inside. "I'm upset at the situation, not you. What are my options?"

As she hoped, the woman relaxed. "If it were up to me, we'd ignore it, but someone filed an anonymous complaint. You need to tear it out or cover it up, and soon, before an inspector drops by."

"I was just inspected for the improvement loan. Why would they come back?"

"Because of that complaint." The woman exhaled slowly through her nose. "There are things I'd actually like to get done, but this is what the county checks on. If we get a complaint, we have to respond."

Deborah left the zoning office ready to start a fistfight.

Which meant she had to stand still a good long time when she got home and found the county inspector already there, pasting a notice on her door that her license to rent units had been revoked.

• • •

Then the Big Bad Development Company came for the house of vinyl.

•••

Thi sat in her foyer, under her prized green wall, patchy with tiny tender buds. The scent of green and the gentle trickle of her new fountain gave the room the sense of a peaceful grotto. She focused on that as the real estate agent refused to leave.

Thi repeated herself. Calmly. "But it's not for sale."

"Did you know your property taxes are set to triple? There's a new law about multifamily dwellings in the area." She laid out papers with delight, like new costs and fees were appetizers. "I hope you don't mind, but we did a teeny credit check and given your current state of indebtedness, here's how much you're expected to lose in the first year." She held out a pen. "Just sign, and it won't be your problem anymore!"

It looked grim, but Thi had never walked away from an investment in her young life. "You're offering less than I paid!"

"Just sign," the woman said, her professional smile straining at the edges.

Thi folded her arms. "I need to show these to my lawyer first."

The woman gathered up all her papers. "No need. Have your lawyer call us directly. Here's my card."

The next day, Thi got a call that her garbage service was cancelled—the city already considered her property sold and uninhabited. The electricity would be cut off at the end of the month.

Thi wondered whom she could have pissed off.

• • •

The Big Bad executives licked their lips at the reports on Thi and Deborah's properties, but most of all they wanted to gobble up the house cobbled together of every sort of thing.

• • •

Gentle was repairing a railing on the fire escape when she was approached by a man in a suede jacket and last year's most popular haircut. "I've been trying to contact the owner of this building," he said. "No one will admit to it! Can you believe that? Who *is* Hessler House, LLC, anyway?"

"We all are." Something about him made Gentle want to say as little as possible. "It's a collective. Every resident is also the owner."

He smiled hungrily. "Could you provide me with a list of contact names?"

"We don't give out that information. At all." Gentle picked up her tools, leaving the repair undone. "Goodbye."

He stuck his arm in the door after her. "You're obviously some form of superintendent …"

She turned to block his entry with her body. "The house manager is in charge of repairs and maintenance. Do you want to talk to the head of the outreach committee? Or our business manager?"

He huffed. "My client wants to buy this property. Who do I talk to?"

"No one. This building is never going to be for sale."

He took a step back, nodding as if accepting a challenge. He touched one of the water-retention posts. "Interesting column you have here."

"It's decorative." Gentle spoke too quickly.

He knocked on the plastic. The sound was undeniably the sound of a water-full drum. "Hm. Is this an approved material for structural elements in Cuyahoga County?"

"Get off our property or we'll call the police."

He tucked a business card between a support and the column. "Get your commies together and consider calling me. It'd be a shame if the building had to be evacuated because it was condemned."

• • •

The three little buildings each felt alone in the face of a massive, mysterious enemy, but they were already linked. Deborah searched her green-architecture enthusiasts group for other owners of older properties in Cleveland, and found Hessler House quickly. Thi searched for property owners in the Cleveland area who had sued against arbitrary rule changes and won, and also found Hessler House.

Which was why, as Gentle sat down with her business manager to learn all she could about this wolfish developer, her phone buzzed with two incoming calls from names she did not recognize.

Because being named "Gentle Rain" made her particularly fond of people whose names were also unusual, and she did not know enough Vietnamese people to know that "Thi" was a common first name, she answered Thi's call first.

Thi stumbled over her words. "Hi, you don't know me, but I'm looking for help and advice."

"Hessler House has an online toolkit to help you start your own collective," Gentle said, and would have hung up if it weren't for the next question.

"Have you heard of a real-estate firm called Big Bad Development?"

Gentle had, minutes ago, found references to just that company. She felt a frisson, as if about to turn the page on a murder mystery. She needed to slow herself down. "Can you hold for a second?" Gentle held up a finger to her business manager, a human-rights lawyer named Prudence Lee, and picked up the other call.

Deborah charged into her words forcefully. "My name is Deborah Harris. We both own older buildings with wastewater reclamation systems. Someone is trying to tell me that's not allowed when I know it is! I think they're trying to strong-arm me out of business. There's this Big Bad Development Company asking to buy me out, and they sure showed up fast. I need to know what I can do, and I think you can help."

Gentle set her phone down and set it to speaker, and conferenced the two calls. "Ladies, I think we should all meet," she said, "How quickly can you get to Hessler Street?"

• • •

Big Bad Company did not know the three little buildings were united. It didn't need to. It was a corporation. The machinations against the three little buildings were not so much orchestrated as churned out, a script calling other scripts. File this, require that, demand the other thing.

Mercilessly, the filings and demands pushed against the poor little arcologies, enlisting the electric company, the sewer company, the police. The outer-ring suburbs had decades of clever little rules that were designed to get rid of neighbours if you didn't like how they trimmed their hedges or the colour of their children.

Thi had to dismantle the green wall. The sections leaned against the porch railings of one of Deborah's units and Thi touched each plant, as though apologizing to it. "All the work I put into that house, and they just took it."

Watching her made Deborah nervous. "You're welcome to stay, until we both get kicked out. I can't collect rent. I don't know what I'm going to do when the taxes come due."

"We'll figure something out." Thi didn't sound sure. She stepped back, her arms at her sides. "We just have to keep them alive."

Deborah wasn't sure she meant the plants. She went into the front room of the apartment, where Gentle frowned fiercely at her laptop. "Any ideas? Because right now, I'm looking at maybe two months I can keep going, then I'll have to declare bankruptcy and lose the building. Do you have room for all these plants in Hessler House?"

Gentle said, "I'm thinking about my business-school days. Corporations rely on quarterly reports to see if their schemes are working, and managers are motivated to make it seem like they are, even when they aren't."

"What good does that do us?" Thi came in with an orchid clutched to her chest.

Deborah frowned. "She means they're slow to react."

Gentle said, "We need to hit them hard and fast, before they know it's coming."

Thi gestured around the empty apartment. "With what?"

Gentle shrugged.

Deborah sat down next to Gentle and got out her phone. "Let's find out together."

They worked late into the night and all weekend, splitting coffee and pizzas. They learned the correct official to reverse a decision and which judge had lost a home to the redevelopment of his block.

Big Bad Company hardly noticed, but that was OK.

You see, this isn't the story about one building surviving because it was strongest. It's the story of how they joined together to all be strong, regardless of what they were made of.

Deborah used Hessler House's legal precedents in her battle to keep her water recycler. Thi used Deborah's contacts to fight the multifamily-rules changes and reverse her eviction. Gentle used Thi's contacts to get Hessler's water collection system labelled an art installation.

Big Bad Company attacked in new ways, but the three little arcologies struggled along, almost but not quite winning, alive in a tie.

And then Thi met Cam, who lived in the next suburb

over and had run into shocking trouble with her solar roof installation, and Deborah met George, who was trying to renovate a series of row houses, and George introduced them all to Wallace, who turned out to know someone Gentle knew, and on and on until the three little arcologies grew into one big community.

Now that there were many hands to lighten the load, they started filing injunctions against Big Bad's properties, and calling in tips to homeowners' associations, and being Big Bad right back.

Big Bad Company noticed, as predicted, only when it was too late. Its middle managers blamed each other and worked to show each other how their part of the corporation was just fine, actually, which was a big help.

And so, after many years, two weddings, and a hundred potlucks, the three little buildings gobbled up the wolfish development company, and they all lived sustainably ever after.

The End.

ABOUT THE AUTHOR

Marie Vibbert has sold over 70 short stories, dozens of poems, and a few comics and computer games. Her debut novel, *Galactic Hellcats*, was released in 2021, about a female biker gang in outer space rescuing a gay prince. By day she is a computer programmer in Cleveland, Ohio.

BOUNDARIES

Cara Mast

IT'S a long swim from the Border Protection Substation down to where the incursion was called in. But Qell's away from her console, ignoring the fifth in a series of Hookd messages she's been avoiding, so the journey down the water column is almost a relief. She has a job to do. And she and her partner Miirn are, in fact, professionals.

Qell knows she's close when the cold seeps past her scales, into her tailbones. And then she sees the infrared signatures of the disrupted locals. The swarming squid don't mind the cold, but they very much mind whatever it is they have surrounded. A break in the swarm reveals the problem, as a much brighter centre flares in Qell's vision. She cracks open a more light-sensitive pair of her eight eyes to confirm, and the blaze of toplight is all she needs to know about this border protection issue.

Miirn slaps one of zir metal arms against the side of

Qell's head and conducts through her skull, "One of them. Damn. Third time this season."

Qell nods. This is getting annoying. Especially since it reminds her of those unanswered messages.

"I'll draw off the locals," Miirn conducts. Ze unwraps the rest of zir arms from around Qell's torso and swims away, lighting up in infrared like a hydrothermal vent a few tails away from Qell and the interloper. The squid follow; they know the patrol's heat signatures. Several swim for Miirn's conductors, trying to make their protests to the robot.

The glass-hooded invader holds up their hands as they paint Qell with toplight.

Qell closes all of her eyes to block the assault of light, fumbles in her patrol belt for her shade-lenses. As she fits the goggles over her topside-eyes, she exhales her annoyance, and her vision clouds briefly with bubbles from her gills. The bubbles glitter in the unnatural light here in the deep, like a veil of stars. And then the bubbles pass and Qell glares properly at the human in the pressure suit.

The pressure suit is an array of lights: yellow floodlights on the shoulders of the suit and red signal lights down one arm and leg, green down the other side. The reinforced "glass" of the suit's hood is lit from within, throwing the human's brown skin and angled face into sharp relief. They set their eyes on Qell. But then the human's eyes widen, flick off to the left.

Qell is not impressed. She waits. Soon, Miirn slides over with a spin of zir many metal arms and climbs once more onto her back. Only four arms secure her partner's body to her own; Miirn presses two of zir arms to the sides of Qell's head, and drapes zir extending arms over her shoulders. Qell kicks her tail once and gets nearly chest-to-chest with the human.

The human blinks rapidly, trying to hide panic as Miirn reaches out and connects zir extending arms to the regulation-required speaker ports on the glass hood. Qell scowls. What was this human expecting, crossing through several border zones without the proper approvals? Any human allowed beyond the sunlight zone has to learn all of the regulations for border crossings because that's what keeps them safe down here.

"I am conducting and projecting," Miirn says. "Please confirm reception."

Qell waits for the human to nod behind their glass. She nods sharply as well, and pulls her communication mask from her patrol belt, fitting it over her nose and mouth. So that she can give yet another border violation speech.

"Qell, your voicebox is connected," Miirn conducts. "You can proceed to ream out this drowner."

Ze sounds extra bitter about this one, so Qell can only imagine what the squid said. Then again, maybe Miirn was busy with something back at the station, rather than waiting for a distraction like she had been. Qell frowns at the intruder. She doesn't know how her species somehow ended up with all of the good sense when they diverged from humanity.

"Human, state your name," Qell says.

"Doctor Aisha Dasher." No excuses, no rushed apology. Qell is instantly suspicious.

"Dr. Dasher, you are in violation of the Oceanic Border Regulations. You are under arrest by Oceanic Border Patrol Officers Qell Oyaoona and Miirn Aquabot. Based on our depth at present, you are multiply in violation, as you have passed through two borders without the appropriate research approvals. Officer Miirn has taken statements from the local population that you disturbed. You have the right to withhold statement until you are delivered to Border Protection Surface Station."

Qell shifts her tail in the cold water, trying not to grimace in discomfort. Why did this one have to come all the way down to the abyssopelagic zone? Especially during this shift, when she and Miirn are the only pair rated for this depth.

Dasher bites their bottom lip, then says, "Can I make an unofficial statement?"

Miirn conducts a curious beep to Qell, then ze projects to the human, "Dr. Dasher, please note that your statement will not be considered unofficial if it is deemed a matter of oceanic security."

"Definitely not a matter of oceanic security. No illegal research was conducted in my descent." Dasher pauses, then adds, "You can check my suit logs."

"I will," Miirn says crisply. Ze conducts to Qell, "You think it's …"

Dasher says, "Qell, Director Margaret is still waiting for

your response."

Miirn laughs at that, conducting to Qell at a volume that Qell thinks is unnecessary. Qell's gills flare and Miirn laughs more rapidly. This is so embarrassing. She knows that she's been avoiding responding to Margaret's last Hookd app message, but she doesn't know what to say. She hates saying no, but she doesn't *want* to say yes to Margaret's latest invitation. Qell wishes she could tag this human for extraction by another team and swim away; border violations are not supposed to be personal issues for border patrol agents.

"You're another one of Margaret's?" Qell says. "That woman is a drought on my gills!"

"She wouldn't keep sending us down here if you would just meet with her, as requested."

Qell growls into the communications mask. "Wave-walking Christ, if that woman wants to speak with me, she could try not breaking wetlaw to do it! Is patience no longer a virtue?"

"She says she wouldn't have to break the law if you would just surface for her." Dasher isn't quite grinning, but they look far more smug than someone under arrest has any right to. "Director Margaret is willing to meet at a venue of your choosing."

"I … Tell Margaret to stop sending people down here; she's going to get me in trouble with my superiors, and she's definitely going to get fined, and possibly given a research moratorium period if she's unlucky."

Qell takes Dasher by one arm and slowly swims up. The human is courteous enough to dim most of their suit lights when Miirn disengages from their helmet, allowing Qell to remove her shade-lenses, and they initiate their suit's propulsion to assist in the slow ascent. Qell is still enough of a professional not to give Dr. Dasher punitive bends by rushing to the surface.

"Border Protection Surface Station is on its way, should be waiting for us when we get topside," Miirn conducts. "By the time we get done with processing, our shift will probably be over!"

Qell doesn't respond. She just keeps looking up, switching eyes as they move up the water column, changing ocean layers, crossing boundaries. The sea life changes as they go: deep invertebrates transitioning to the red and black bathypelagic fish, to the silvery creatures of the twilight zone, up to the blues and greens of the near-surface swimmers. All beautiful in their own ways. All curious about the border patrol escort of a human. By the time they're in the light zone, Qell is flushed hot, and not just because the water is so much warmer up here.

Miirn is correct in zir assessment; getting through Dr. Dasher's booking and paperwork, plus their end-of-watch report, takes Qell and Miirn straight to clocking out. Right before Miirn unfolds from Qell's back to go to dock, ze taps zir arms against the back of Qell's head.

"See, Qell? I told you dating apps are fun!"

Qell sighs out of her gills again, shaking her head through

the cloud of bubbles, not willing to debate Miirn on zir definition of fun. She pulls her commscreen from her civilian vest pocket, opens Hookd to reread Margaret's last message. Deletes that, and the other four messages. Blocks Margaret on the app.

Let it never be said that an Oceanic Border Patrol Officer doesn't know how to enforce a boundary.

ABOUT THE AUTHOR

As a retired tall-ship sailor, a failed academic, and a millennial finance professional, Cara gets stopped constantly in New York City and asked for directions. Cara spends their free time drinking coffee, binging words, and yelling about the Philadelphia Eagles in their apartment and family group chat. They can be found on twitter @digicara, and at digicara.com.

LOST BEYOND THE LIGHTS

P. A. Cornell

"WAKE up, Paola, it's time."

My daughter shifts in her bed in a way that reminds me of when she was a child, but she has children of her own now—the oldest a teenager already. How did so many years pass so quickly? Tonight, my own childhood seems close enough to touch, the echoes of another night just like this one rippling through time to connect with this very moment.

"Despierta, ya es hora," I hear my own father's voice, waking me all those years ago for the same reason, though unlike Paola I was just a boy then, barely ten years old.

"What time is it?" she asks, back in the present.

"Nearly three in the morning," I say. "Time to go see the comet. Help me wake the kids. We have to get going if we're going to beat the dawn."

She gets up and I give her a moment to dress. Then together we go to her children's rooms and wake them one by one. Sebastián, the sixteen-year-old, wakes easily and manages to get himself ready, but the twins, Miguel and Mariana, don't truly wake completely. They're just barely alert enough for us to help them dress. This again reminds me of when their mother was little. Once they're ready, we take them to the car, where all three kids fall back asleep.

"Might as well let them get some rest," I say. "We'll still have to drive for a while if we're going to see anything."

I notice Paola looking up into the sky.

"Which direction do we have to look in?"

I laugh. "Don't bother trying here. The lights of Santiago are too bright to let us see much of anything. That's why we have to drive out of the city. In the darkness of the countryside, we'll see more clearly."

We get in the car and Paola falls asleep like the children. I look at her and remember how excited she would get about new experiences when she was a girl. I couldn't have gone without her tonight. She's a grown woman but she's still my girl and like any parent I want to see the wonder on her face, just as much as I want to see my grandchildren delight in this rare opportunity.

I switch the car from self-driving to manual and take control of our journey. As I drive, I think about the last time Halley's Comet paid a visit. We were living in Santiago then too, so my father also had to drive us out of the city so that we could see past the glare of electric lighting. It was a much shorter drive in those days though. I'll have to go much farther due to the city's growth in the decades since.

As I drive, I can't help but wonder how the wildlife has fared with this increase in brightness. Not only has the growth of the city encroached on habitats, but near the city there is no true night left either. How do the animals hide from predators? How do they make their way through life blinded by our selfish need to see at all hours?

It's not long before I pass the area known as Lo Barnechea, at the foot of the Andes. I think back to that night again, my father telling me that just as we could see the comet from Earth, you could see La Cordillera de los Andes from space. It was to this very place that he brought us. But back then the area was rural and teeming with life. Now it's built up like the rest of Santiago and it's hard to mesh with the memories I have of that night. So, I keep going.

I've reached the age where memory is an elusive thing. But somehow my memories of the first time I saw the comet are fresh as the night air. I remember walking through a field so dark you could only see the small circle of light cast by my father's flashlight. But then the clouds cleared and suddenly the sky above came to life. A city kid through-and-through, I stood in awe. I'd never seen so many stars. The full Milky Way was on display as if specifically for us. And then my father had pointed out the comet, hanging in the sky as if someone had nailed it up there.

My father had brought along an old pair of binoculars. My brothers and I took turns looking through them. Though we could see the comet without them, the binoculars brought it even closer so that you could make out the details and almost imagine that you could see its movement.

We'd learned about Halley's Comet in school that year. How it passed by Earth every seventy-five years or so. How it was named after Edmond Halley, a British astronomer. There'd even been an awful song written and performed by some one-hit-wonder that had played over and over on the radio. Every school kid knew the words and sang it ad nauseum, me included. But seeing the comet—actually *seeing* it in real life—had been a completely different thing. There are few moments in life when you realize you're living through something you'll remember forever, but for me, that night, I just knew.

When we'd all had a turn at the binoculars, we lay back in the grass and watched the sky for a long time. I remember telling my brother, "We could still be alive when it comes back again. If I am, I'll come back here with my kids and grandkids so they can see it too."

I think about that now as I drive further from Lo Barnechea. The location will have to be different this time, but my younger self would let that slide since the aim remains the same.

With the glow of the city finally fading behind us, I figure we've gone far enough. I can't keep driving forever, after all, or the sun will rise and the moment will be lost. I pull the car off the road and park in what looks like a valley, surrounded by smallish hills that help block some of the city light. It seems like a good spot.

"Paola," I say, shaking my daughter awake. "We're here."

She helps me wake the children and then the five of us head for one of the hills, looking for a higher spot from which we might better see the wonders of the night sky. There's some cloud cover for now but it's supposed to clear up soon, so I'm not too concerned. I carry with me my telescope—a piece of equipment my father would have envied. On a clear night, Halley's Comet is visible with the naked eye, but with these old eyes I don't want to take any chances.

We reach the top of the small hill and still can't see much, but I can feel the steady breeze and can already see the clouds above begin to part. I turn now to Paola and the kids. I want to see their faces when the stars are revealed. Paola is pointing her flashlight at the ground so as not to ruin the effect, but I can still make out her smile as she looks at me, then switches it off.

The clouds part but the sky is filled with an unexpected brightness. Far off in the distance I see sky adverts. Glowing, orbiting billboards projected into the night sky. There are half a dozen visible from this spot. Ads for shoes, smart-home systems, a discount on lab-grown meat that boasts of its superior flavour. I raise my telescope and strain to see past the adverts.

Around them I can just make out the faint glow of a scattering of the brightest stars, but that's it. And just at the edge of the shoe advert, there's a smudge that could possibly be Halley's Comet, but it's too hard to see.

"Where's the comet, *abuelito*?" asks Mariana.

"Let me try, *Papá*," Paola says, handing me the flashlight to take the telescope. She searches the sky with her younger eyes.

I take a moment to look at my grandchildren. They huddle together against the biting chill of the night and the little ones yawn. They're bored. This wasn't what I wanted.

"I don't see anything," Sebastián says. "Can we go home now? I'm tired."

Paola lowers the telescope and looks at me, her expression sad.

"Maybe we just need to drive a little further out," she suggests.

I shake my head. "I thought this far out of Santiago we might get a spot of clear sky, but it looks like we can never get far enough away to be free of those damn adverts."

Like most people, I'd heard about the light-pollution problem but I hadn't given it much thought until now. In the city it didn't matter. The light made the night easier to get around in. But now, it hits home just how bad things have gotten.

Chile was once a paradise for astronomers. They'd come from all over the world to study the wonders of space. But in recent years several of our famed observatories have shut down. I'd read the news reports but they hadn't affected me. Not until this very moment.

"We could drive halfway to San Pedro de Atacama and it

wouldn't make a difference," I tell Paola. "I doubt even the desert is free of these eyesores."

"Let's go home then," says Miguel. "I'm cold."

The kids turn and begin walking back toward the car. Paola takes the flashlight back from me and returns the telescope.

"*Lo siento Papá*," she says. "I know you wanted to see the comet again. I'm so sorry."

She turns and follows the kids, shining the light toward them.

I raise the telescope to the sky one last time, but still can't see much of anything besides the adverts. Paola's sadness is misplaced though. I did want to see the comet once more, but my real reason for coming was so that they could see it. After all, I have my memories and can see it clearly there any time I want to.

But they will never have that. They will never know what was lost behind bright lights.

ABOUT THE AUTHOR

P.A. Cornell is a Chilean-Canadian speculative fiction writer. She currently lives in Canada, but was living in Santiago, Chile during the mid-80s where late one night her father took her to the outskirts of the city to see Halley's Comet, an event that over thirty years later would inspire this story. A member of SFWA and graduate of the Odyssey workshop, her short fiction has appeared in several professional anthologies and genre magazines. For a full bibliography and social media links, visit pacornell.com.

UPHILL BOTH WAYS IN THE SNOW

Sheila Jenné

"Do I really have to be here for this?" said the finance minister, sweat rolling down his round face as they trudged across the shimmering tarmac.

"You could let the rest of us talk to him and cut you out of the negotiations," said the agriculture minister.

"Nobody's getting cut out of anything," said State. She was an elegant woman with hair as white as snow, or as white as snow used to be.

"It just galls, asking a colonial for help," complained Finance. "*We're* supposed to be helping *them*. A generation ago, we helped them all the time."

"That's why they owe us, wouldn't you say?" said Agriculture. He was bronzed and handsome, impeccably dressed in a pinstripe suit, with a cowboy hat to still look like a farmer. "I'm hoping they see it that way."

"We hardly have any other options," said State. "We wouldn't have asked him to come if we did."

The Martian delegate was already climbing down out of his shuttle, a lean and lanky figure with grey hair flopping over his face.

"Welcome to Earth, sir," said State, raising her hand in greeting. "Respirator?"

The Martian scoffed. "Respirator? In this atmosphere? When I was a kid we had half a percent of cee oh two and didn't make a fuss about it." But he took the breather and slapped it on with a practiced hand.

They picked their way back across the airstrip to the little building designated for the meeting. "I'm frankly embarrassed to have you here," said Finance, puffing a little as he hung up his respirator. "Earth is a mess."

"'S why I'm here," said the Martian amiably, taking a seat. "You wanted Mars's help with your little atmosphere problem?"

"It's not a *little* problem," said State, opening a folder and laying out a number of papers, detailing carbon dioxide levels, temperature trends, and sea level rise. "By our estimation, we have only decades before Earth becomes uninhabitable."

The Martian peered at the papers, pooching out his lips. "You know, it was only decades *ago* that Mars was uninhabitable."

"Yes, we felt you would be able to understand our plight." State gave a gentle smile, the one she saved for reassuring citizens in times of crisis. In recent years it had gotten a lot of mileage.

The Martian pushed the papers back across the table. "Then you asked the wrong planet. I grew up in a tunnel, lady. I breathed wild air for the first time when I was ten years old. And then we had a cold winter and the Northern Ocean algae mat died off, and the amount of carbon dioxide released made the air toxic for another ten years."

Finance leaned forward, his round face eager. "So what did you do?"

"We started wearing breathers again and we engineered cold-resistant algae. Terraforming isn't a fun little exercise for babies. It's work and there are setbacks every year. The important thing is that we never stop trending the right way."

State frowned. "We're *not* trending the right way."

The Martian stabbed a finger at her. "That," he said, "that's your problem there. Not any of this stuff."

"I'm pretty sure these things are problems as well!" insisted Finance, pulling a paper toward him. "Look at these hurricanes, they're increasing—" he squinted at the chart on the paper—"a lot!"

"Storms?" said the Martian. "As our terraforming project goes on, every year the weather is some different wild thing. Till the levels are constant, y'see, it's not gonna settle down. One time I had to go to work in a dust storm so bad you couldn't see your hand in front of your face. People can survive storms."

"Storms kill people!" snapped Agriculture.

State turned to the Martian, her face apologetic. "You see, people understating the severity of the problem is what got us into this mess. Everyone said it wasn't going to be a big deal, and the next thing we knew it was too late to fix."

"Is it?" said the Martian. "Too late to fix?"

"The problems are certainly upon us," Agriculture said. "Food production is down, thanks to storms and droughts. We're expecting a 2% shortfall this year. That means 2% of the most vulnerable Earthers are likely to starve."

The Martian narrowed his eyes. "That's not what I get out of the math. 'Bout ten years ago, there was a blight in our rice crop. We all tightened our belts for a while. Kids got first dibs on it. But nobody *starved*."

"On Earth, people starve," State said earnestly. "Every year, a certain number—it's in the dossier."

"Then why don't you *all* eat two percent less?"

There was a silence around the table as the ministers exchanged glances. State pulled a paper toward her, flipped it over, and made a note. "Thank you for your advice, sir."

"Is that what you want here? Advice? I got a lot. I also brought some of our high-yield seeds, algae cultures to sequester the carbon, whatever we have. Of course we don't have anything for your plastics issue, or the atmospheric particulates. But I brought everything we thought would help you. I'll stick around as long as it takes to teach y'all how to use it."

Finance stared at Agriculture, who caught the glance and stared at State. Finally she said, "That's actually not the sort of help we're looking for. I think maybe you underestimate how drastic the damage to our planet is. What we want is some kind of mass refugee status. Our planet is rapidly becoming unlivable. Yours is a paradise. And there's plenty of room— not, maybe, for the whole population of Earth, but for as many as we can hope to get off in time."

The Martian's face darkened. He leaned forward, about to speak, stopped, started again. "You," he said at last, "can fuck off."

State blinked. "Excuse me, sir?"

"You can fuck off into the sun," he clarified. "And then fuck on through it. I don't care.

"My people started with a barren rock and made a paradise. Y'all were given a paradise and turned it into a barren rock. I have no patience with you. I grew up working every minute for my planet. Tending the algae mats in a respirator. Processing sewage to get methane to run systems on while you were all burning dinosaur oil. Going without things I wanted just to make sure every single Martian had enough air and water and food to live on. We carved that paradise out of rock with sweat and blood and tears, and look at you. Look at you!" His gesture took in State's smart suit, Agriculture's hat, Finance's paunch. "You've never gone without a day in your life, and you want me to believe you *can't survive?* You don't *want* to survive."

State's face was flushed. "I assure you, we very much want to survive. The yearly death tolls—"

"You *chose* that," said the Martian. "You could've been

working all this time to prevent that, but no. You trashed this place like a frat house you weren't paying for. And now what's the plan? Y'all and your friends come over to our place and leave everyone else here to foot the bill?"

Finance swallowed. "Perhaps we could find a way to get everyone off—"

"No," said the Martian. "We ain't doing that. We'll take refugees, maybe, but not you. You and your friends will never be welcome, 'cause you're the ones that caused this mess. Any ship comes our way full of rich Earthers and government types? It's getting fired on. I've got my government's approval to say that. They've been paying attention to what y'all have been doing back here."

State shuffled her papers back into a pile, her face pale. "You're sentencing us to death," she said.

"No ma'am. We're sentencing you to growing a pair. Get off your asses and fix your goddamn planet, because there isn't another one for you. You don't get to give up on Earth. We won't let you."

With that he heaved himself to his feet and stomped out of the building. Through the window they could see him trekking across the tarmac alone, barefaced and sweating, back to his rocket.

"He's like my granddad," said Finance, voice quavery with released tension. "'In my day we didn't have these fancy schoolbuses! We had to trek to school uphill, both ways, in the snow!'"

"Shut up," said State.

Agriculture was on his feet, grabbing a respirator at the door. "I'm going after him," he said. "Gonna get those seeds."

ABOUT THE AUTHOR

Sheila Jenné grew up watching Star Trek and reading about spaceships and dragons. Today, she has four young children, a job writing financial advice articles, and an incurable itch to create worlds and galaxies of her own. When she gets a brief break from those callings, she likes to spin yarn, bake, and garden.

STONES OF SÄRDAL

Karl Dandenell

IF you don't mind, I'm going to do this in English. Even though I emigrated here forty years ago, I've never quite mastered the Swedish accent. What can I say? I grew up in America.

Are you sure there's no script? I thought this needs to be educational, like a museum.

Yes, I know there won't be an *actual* museum on the ship. From what I've seen, there's not much *ship* there at all. Just thousands of kilometres of light sail, with one little module in the middle. I imagine a bus being pulled by a kite the size of Utah.

Sorry, I tend to wander, but that's what happens when you're 105. Did you know the queen of Sweden sent me a video on my 100th birthday? Estelle Silvia herself. I still have a copy around here somewhere. Probably upstairs in the junk drawer. You'll have to go look. Those steps are tricky. This house was built by people thirty centimetres shorter than me and they *definitely* didn't understand plumb lines.

Sure, I can talk about the house. Check out the front door —that's original glass. Blown by hand back in 1860 or so. Terrible insulation but so beautiful. In the summer when the sun is going down around 11 p.m. it makes the most amazing shadows and rainbows. When it's hot, we open up the doors and let the breeze come through. It never got that hot when I was a kid. I wore sweaters in the summer, can you believe it? Now it hardly snows even in the winter, except up in Lapland. Too much CO_2 in the atmosphere.

Anyway, the kitchen is right through here. In the morning, the first person out of bed opens up the back door, and props it open with hook and eyebolt. That door stays open from dawn to late night. Everyone sits on the porch and eats and visits. The adults read the news on their tablets and the kids drown their corn flakes in *filmjölk* and fresh *hallon*. Sour milk and raspberries. If you'd come later, we could have had some. But the berries won't be ripe for another few weeks and I know you want to upload this sooner than that.

The house used to belong to a sea captain. That's what folks did around here. They worked the sea. And farmed, though the soil was pretty poor.

That changed by and by. The sea captain died. I don't know if he drowned or got captured by pirates or eaten by one of those moose that sometimes swim over from Denmark. Anyway, the captain's widow had nothing except this house. Rather than sell it, she turned it into an inn. And a speakeasy. That's an unlicensed drinking spot, if you don't know. From all accounts it was very popular, and she made enough to get by, and a little bit more. *Lagom*.

Let's walk around the corner. There's the outdoor shower, wooden walls and half open to the wind. It's no big deal now but when my mother was a kid this was one of the few summer houses to have plumbing like that, and we were able to hold on to our water rights during the droughts. A lot of folks lost theirs and had to move away. Can't live here unless you were willing to pay the community for desalination. More *kronor* than I've got, let me tell you. But at least we have the option. Half of Europe is on water rations last I heard.

Okay, look over there, toward the ocean. That little shack. That's a lifeboat museum. Well, it used to be. Big storm knocked it down a few years ago, clawing back about five metres of beach at the same time. Everyone says we were lucky my *mormor* had planted all these birch trees as a wind break.

And do you see that line of rocks? That used to be a quay. The ships would tie up there when the sailors came to the speakeasy. Those were beautiful ships, with brilliant white sails, if the painting in the sitting room is at all accurate. The ships plied the Baltic between here and Denmark and Germany. When they put in, they did a little trading. Loaded up on smoked meat and good iron tools. And stones. You heard me. Stones. The beach was lousy with them, and the ships would dump their ballast, which was soil, and take on stones.

Why? They *sold* them. For cobblestones. If you go down to the historical districts in Copenhagen or Greifswald, you're walking on stones from this very beach. From Särdal.

And the soil they left behind? My ancestors carted that off to those fields behind those houses. Mixed it in with the local dirt and planted potatoes. The best in Sweden. Ask anyone. All because some traders wanted a drink and some cobblestones.

I almost forgot—I have something for you. Here's a pebble I dug out of the garden. It looks like a face, doesn't it? Like a baby with its eyes closed. That's good luck. Please, take it.

Listen, I know every gram is precious on the spaceship. There's no room for people, just androids and the seed stock and the cloning tanks.

And stories.

But that little ship will be sailing those starry seas for decades.

They could use a little luck.

Take the pebble.

ABOUT THE AUTHOR

Karl Dandenell is a graduate of Viable Paradise and a Full Member of the Science Fiction Writers of America. He and his family, plus their cat overlords, live on an island near San Francisco famous for its Victorian architecture and low-speed traffic. His preferred drinks are strong Swedish tea and distilled spirits, neat.

Karl's work has appeared in such publications as *Fireside Fiction*, *Buzzy Magazine*, *Metaphorosis*, *Speculative North*, and the anthologies *Abandoned Places* and *Strange Economics*.

EM ONTVLECETV / INVADED

Deidra Suwanee Dees

YOU invaded my space with anticlimactic explosion,
you singed my tongue with a new breed of speech,
Vhopvketv Muscogee dances descend upon erosion,
how can you still drive me into retreat?

daddy fought with you in the Jewish holocaust
making me believe your heart holds empathy,
Opunvkv my polluted Mother is almost lost,
why can't I convince you to believe in me?

when Muscogees ruled, we had enough to eat,
children went to sleep at night in a safe place,
Enokketv there were no radiated rivers nor COVID disease,
but now you behold an emaciated race;

vanishing land that belonged to me,

I am the essence of a dying turtle's call,

Somketv you've stolen everything—*even my dignity*,

how can you hurt me more when I've already lost it all?

ABOUT THE AUTHOR

Dr. Deidra Suwanee Dees is the Director/Tribal Archivist at the Poarch Band of Creek Indians in the U.S. State of Alabama. In her second job, she teaches in the Native American Studies Program at the University of South Alabama which was initiated by the 2014 sponsorship of the Tribe. She earned her doctorate at Harvard, writing her dissertation on the *Muscogee Education Movement* which documents Creeks' turbulent sociopolitical journey to achieve equal access to public education from 1928-49. She is deeply in love with Mother Earth and sends *heleswv heres* (good medicine) to the people of Mother Earth. *Mvto.*

THE ENDERS

Maria S. Picone

I was twelve when they descended into the alleys where I played with my brother. They called themselves the Enders; back then, we didn't know what it implied. Tall gleaming creatures with perfect teeth, they seemed made of sun and sky, destined to shed light on our brown-skinned existence, lowly as the earth at night. Awestruck, we buzzed with the minutiae of their lives. "The one named Jason"—my brother said this like "chase on"—"he is from 'Ohio'"—spoken like the Japanese おはよう.

Though they asked me my name, I saw their eyes go slack like calm oceans as I repeated it. "You can be Janet, like my girl back home," a kind one said.

I crammed the name in my mouth like a Hershey's Bar. "Cha-nes."

They called my brother Sergeant Pepper, joking that they were his "band." They taught him how to sing, "It's wonderful to be here/It's certainly a thrill." He learned to recite the entire duty roster. Since our parents' deaths, he was my world. I became "Janet" for him.

The Enders built roads, factories, and buildings, articulating their civilization over acres of claimed territory. Their language seeded in like weeds as we realized we had been speaking wrong all along. We harvested their discards: frizzed out toasters, T-shirts with wisdom like *Bob's Burgers Are the Best in Town* and *Life Ain't Worth Livin' Without A Boat!*, faded backpacks stamped with their straight-sky-line alphabet. Our writing crept along the undergrowth in curls and blossoms; theirs reached to the cosmos and weaponized the sun, the stars, even the round and smiling moon. My brother and I tossed a sparkling, bouncing ball they gave us back and forth until it rolled into the road one morning and burst at the seams like a bomb.

• • •

Eventually, the Enders gave up on building into the city, content to remain in their neighbourhood. They still interacted with useful locals—men who knew how to unassertively shake hands, women who wore heels that mustered them up to just under the sky army's arms, children who afforded them a moment of borderless joy. Often, one day's kids became the men and women of the next. Like us. I worked at a restaurant for Ender clientele, offering hampurgers and nostellgia in maladroit English. I slipped in an army private between my shifts. We met over onnion rings. He was clean-shaven and never paid me, which was enough.

My brother, who went by Sarge, never got over his appreciation of the Enders, graduating from the school of Awe of Them and into the school of Money off Them. When he came home at dawn, he smelled of a thousand varietals of cigarettes. He told me the Enders built whole cities from good Midwestern steel. "You don't understand, Janet," he said. "Imagine the technology we'll have in fifty years!" I swallowed a frown, but I couldn't express the unsettled quiet in my chest. He said our scaffolded city didn't approach the high towers of places whose names I could now pronounce: Pittsburgh, Detroit, Cleveland. Had I paid attention to the sinister shadows—"pits," "destroy," "cleave"—I would have known the Enders were rapacious for the fresh fruits of our language, our familial wisdom, even the unspoiled wilderness of our culture. They knew how to make a false beginning, but their talents lay in eating. In the downfall of our people, they ate and ate well.

• • •

I was nineteen and a half when smog greyed out the sky. The ground lightened like a girl who used whitening cream. The neighbourhood mobilized with speculation. When we went to the Enders and begged for rain, they shot bullets into the sky. These wheeled like beehives and pollinated the earth with pink-magenta blood. Everyone knew this was the colour blood should be.

Pursuant to this, the Enders began shooting every problem. The Ender homeland sent relief aid of various calibres. There were so many guns the Enders started tipping with them, leaving M9s next to the extra bite of bun marooned by their burger patty. A drunken patron shipping out on the next helicopter gave me an M4 carbine. That was a good day. Sometimes I thought myself incapable of another degree of grief. And then I would find it: another lake flooding with jellyfish tendrils of plastic. Another ambitious child who scraped the heavens and fell.

At work, I often heard "it's *wonderful* to be here" from natives and Enders alike. My private confided to our M4 that he was thinking about leaving me. When he hugged me, his arms felt reinforced, like steel struts. I cried into my pillow and pretended not to hear the clack-clack-clack of the trigger as he used the bathroom. Tips stopped coming, except for hollow bullet casings. The quiet in my heart thickened like polluted water, leaving me poisoned, gasping, weak. Everyone talked about getting out. Even my brother told me he thought he could make a deal. Our arguments ruptured our universe. But I refused to leave our parents' grief site.

• • •

When they opted to End, I almost felt better. Everyone knew this was the way our country should be. They firebombed their base of operations and smote the hamburgers and nostalgia that I served. They redlined our cities, turning water to blood, crimson and merciful like Jesus asked. Helicopters wheeled like camo crows, carrying the Enders to their next civilization.

My brother and I took shelter inside an old shrine. There, in the embrace of ancestors, we waited; to survive, we pressed the fruits of our people to our ignorant mouths. Eventually, the sun, the stars, even the hungry rattling moon departed; all that was left was shadow upon shadow.

The clouds burst like bombs overhead. We felt the groans of hard rain—we closed our eyes and reached for each other's hands. After years of silence, the relief of our own language crept in. I whispered my brother's real name.

ABOUT THE AUTHOR

Maria S. Picone is a Korean American adoptee who won *Cream City Review*'s 2020 Summer Poetry Prize. She has been published in *Ice Floe Press*, *Bending Genres*, *Whale Road Review*, and more, including *Best Small Fictions 2021*. She has received grants from *Kenyon Review*, Lighthouse Writers, GrubStreet, The Watering Hole, SAFTA, The Speakeasy Project, and others. She is the prose editor at *Chestnut Review*, poetry editor at *The Hanok Review*, associate editor at *Uncharted Mag*, and managing editor at *Emerge Literary Journal*. Her work explores hybridity, social justice, and pop culture. Her website is mariaspicone.com, Twitter @mspicone.

FLIGHT OF THE STORM GOD

Mike Adamson

SOMETIMES the dreams are wonderful, and sometimes they are living hell.

There are times I walk in the Eden of olden times, when the world was green and the wind made racing waves across the steppes. I was there not long ago, it seems, standing in the clean wind under a warm sun, looking across the land, rolling away to the spine of the Urals—the mountains that bisect Europe from Asia—white against the sky. I could forget for a while the reality of matters, luxuriate in the sense of the primal Earth, its air so kind upon my skin. There were birds on the wing, horses upon the green sea, and the world was good.

I remember those dreams fondly, and know the AI tries valiantly to foster such memories, to damp down the nightmares—for when they break through it seems they endure for months, years, and my sanity staggers in the grip of images I would sooner forget. Only when I am fully conscious can I deal with reality by a philosophic feat, for who could endure the ongoing vision of those green lands made desert, dunes where there had been rivers, a world of stinging wind filled with grit, and where the cities of old were swallowed down deep by the marching sands?

Heat and dust now define Earth, a scorching planet with a broken food web and largely dead oceans. Only the tropical forests persist in the carbon-dioxide-rich air. The oceans encroached upon the coastal plains, 130 metres of onlap worked its relentless destruction upon the doings of humankind, and cities above those elevations are eerie necropoli filled with the bleached bones of billions.

I think it was this horror, more than any other aspect, that taxed my sanity in the endless night of waiting. The AI bridge into my consciousness was linked via the dream cortex, and those dreams dominated me in ways they were never meant to. A clean passage through the alpha brainwave range as I ascended to consciousness or down into the untroubled sleep of ages would have made the process simple, but actually waking was something I could never do.

None of us could, we, the 29,000 souls who survived here.

That was the trick, coming close enough to consciousness for my mind to be in control of itself without my physical body actually waking; the infiltration of dreams was the price, and technicians long ago had warned me I risked madness. But someone must be aware of the world to make the decision to wake, and as director of the project I would leave the task to no other.

How long? The AI whispered to me of decades flowing by, of conditions above slowly changing. Forty years ago it noticed an anomaly on the external visual pickups and correlated observations to reach the astonishing conclusion that energy reaching the ground from the sun had fractionally reduced, as if solar output had lessened. No known mechanism could account for it but recalculation now assumed a slow but genuine cooling trend in our over-hot world.

As the hundred drones went about their repetitive tasks, maintaining the biostasis modules, I saw through their eyes, walked the chill corridors of the redoubt, and consoled myself with the thought that all was *in the green*—we were alive, and would stay so for as long as it took. My machine memory told me I had paced the catwalks to their modules— Eleyna and Talia—176 times; each pilgrimage was to stand for a while and look down on their faces, unchanging in the gentle arms of stasis, and heave a mental sigh, longing for the moment the march of the years was over and we would be together again.

One can acclimate to anything, and I had come to understand my lot was eternity, gliding from year to year and decade to decade. Thus it was with strange disquietude I felt myself roused from the deeper layers where dreams came less frequently, piloted up through vivid cycles toward the edges of wakefulness, where my mind could reach through and phase with the world once more.

Things have changed, the AI whispered, *faster than we ever anticipated. The air is breathable once more.*

How—I stammered mentally, but had no time to complete the thought before the real message drove home to me with the force of a cometary impact.

We have visitors.

• • •

Not in more than seven decades had any living thing walked these halls, and I was perturbed by the thought of coming face to face with whoever it may be.

I phased in a smooth, cool dive into the perceptive envelope of a maintenance drone, breathed mentally as if I still had a body of flesh and blood, and flexed powerful metal hands. My vision cleared and I knew at once I was in submaintenance bay twelve, the machine vault where the drones repaired each other. No lights were required, my senses were multiple layers of thermoscan and lidar, supplementing empirical knowledge of the redoubt layout. I had an immediate feed via the AI from the external sensors on the energy towers far above, and a passive imaging system fed me a scene such as I had imagined down the long, dark years but never truly dared expect.

The wind-tormented desert was its dirty red-brown self, the slope down to the dry meanders of the Ural River, here to the west of lost Orenburg, a rippled field of low dunes. A hundred metres from the slowly corroding towers that rose, squat and obtuse, from the desert, stood a craft of unknown design; wing-mounted engines were obviously rotated for vertical landing performance, and from it had emerged four people.

People!

Human beings—living human beings! My heart flip-flopped and I zoomed the lens to examine them one by one. Two men, two women—a tall, broad, Slavic male, a Caucasian male with more western features; one of the women was small, petite and Chinese, the other a flaxen-haired European. This latter was dressed in a rugged jumpsuit of dusty white fabric, the others in what seemed a uniform of simple cut and grey-green tone. They walked with care in the slithery sands, panning instruments as they examined the towers, and I knew at once they had no knowledge of the redoubt—zero information had come down to them, and my curiosity was doubled when I matched this to the mystery of how the external environment had veered back toward human habitable inside the same century as its downfall.

The signal sky was quiet in all the bands we were tuned to monitor, but clearly we had been listening in the wrong regions of the spectrum. These people were technological and appeared healthy enough, healthier than the oxygen-poor air and still high temperatures should have permitted. Perhaps—my digital heart fluttered at this notion—perhaps those who had abandoned Earth had returned at last.

I was unsure how I felt about it, but a current of

resentment made itself known. We had held our ground, cloven to Mother Earth, not run away from the mess our ancestors made. It was *ours* to inherit, and we had every tool and resource in our vast underground chambers to do so when the time was right. But these strangers' presence posed uncomfortable questions, thoughts that placed our survival strategy in doubt, and this was unacceptable.

With a whine of servos I stepped out of the drone's service dock and headed for the vertical access. After a seeming eternity of sleeping darkness, I was back—and before all else I was my people's protector. I rose to a command node on a higher level and woke systems with silent, lightning-fast commands, standing in a ring of projection screens on which data streamed and images played from a dozen perspectives. Here I contented myself to watch; after three-quarters of a century, what did a few hours matter? If they were smart, the visitors would find their way in.

As the day aged toward evening I watched them scanning the towers as if they had no notion of such designs—likely checking for ionizing radiation, and chemo- and biohazards. The structures were merely the upper extremities of a thermal-differential energy installation, whose endlessly circulating freon gas, between the heat of the upper world where it expanded violently and the chill of bedrock where it recondensed, drove generators and provided all the power the redoubt would ever need. It was engineering no more complicated than a refrigerator, but on the scale of a skyscraper, and its sheer simplicity guaranteed longevity. These people from the sky must be looking for something more complex, I guessed, and their perplexity struck me as amusing. But they brought tools from their craft and spent an hour shovelling sand and grit from the base of one of the stacks, and at last uncovered an access hatch.

Now it got interesting and I watched with keen attention as the tall Slav pried open the command panel by the hatch, dismantled the code keypad and scanned the reverse side, obviously analyzing the circuitry. I knew it was just a matter of time before he worked out how to circumvent the entry lockout. I smiled mentally, acknowledging the smarts of our guests, as motors turned for the first time since the complex was sealed, withdrawing tooled steel lugs, and the door swung inward. I felt motion sensors detect the intruders and systems swung into action—LED strips blinked on and fans began to circulate the stale, hot air.

In the sight of discreet cameras, the four penetrated the service way surrounding the heat-exchanger ducting at the core of the tower and began their descent. Now I nodded to myself. It was time. I strode to meet them, aware clearly as they encountered other drones in their rounds, and I ordered the machines to remain impassive at the intrusion.

The long metal halls were chill and echoed dully to footfalls. My sensors picked up voices as I approached, a Russian accent commenting in English as service panels were read: "High-pressure air line ... Condensation recovery duct ... Main A/C harness ... Caution: Hot ... Robot access only ..."

At once the four intruders whirled as I strode purposefully from a turning and eased to a halt before them. The moment was more laden with meaning than even my processors could calculate and I registered their apprehension as they took in my form, head and shoulders taller than any of them, my dull metallic casing stenciled with Cyrillic characters. My optical pickups glowed softly as I scanned them in return, while my human heart sang to behold the living.

"I don't think it's hostile," the Chinese woman whispered after a few moments, and my reaction was a very human twitch of my shoulders.

"Privetstvuyu," I said, amiably enough, to the Slavic man, who smiled at once.

"Zdravstvuyte," he returned easily, as I placed my hands together in human manner.

A moment later I switched languages. "Chinese, Russian, European ... I sense English is your *lingua franca."* I read their expressions and moved on, my voice slightly metallicized and with a soft Russian accent. I spoke easily but with a reserve perhaps only I appreciated. "Welcome to the South Urals Survival Redoubt ... We have waited a *very* long time."

The silence was difficult, and the fair-haired European woman stepped forward. "Doctor Sondra Cullaine, of Prometheus City, out by the moon. I'm in command."

I extended my hand gently and an emotion for which I was not ready filled me as I pronounced my name for the first time. "Doctor Anton Mikhailov. My body lies sleeping with the rest, but my mind is very much here."

With the strangest feelings in my heart and belly, I felt her clasp my cold metal hand, and I shook with a soul from my personal future.

•••

They had torn apart asteroids for the raw materials to build their cities, powered by the sun and the atom, and controlled by EM drives. I wished my drone body was more expressive as I struggled to keep up with the revelations. Using the same technologies, they had placed a vast obstruction in space between sun and Earth, generating an eternal eclipse that mediated in a very controlled way the precise amount of energy striking the planet at any latitude, at any time. This was what the AI had detected decades ago, explaining the trend to a cooler environment. I accepted their explanations, if not uncritically, as the AI surged in its cybernetic vaults, examining the data, crossmatching and modelling.

"Outside oxygen levels are our indicator of the recovery of the planet," I replied as I led our guests along an interminable corridor in the cool depths of the complex. "The redoubt was designed to survive for many centuries if need be. The terrain is geologically reasonably stable, minor disturbances the engineering can cope with. A hundred drones look after the systems and themselves, while the power will flow as long as the heat differential lasts." I paused by a long gallery and passed a hand over a control. Metal window shields ground slowly upward to reveal a vista of systems in multiple repetition—and I felt a hand brush my spine at our guests' expressions as they realized they looked out upon tier after tier of casket-sized capsules.

"Are they biostasis modules?" The European man, Travers, whispered.

"29,000 people lie sleeping below," I replied simply. "When the O_2/CO_2 balance comes even 10% closer to preindustrial levels, it will be time for them to wake and build a new home." I gestured with a hydraulic arm. "There I am, on that uppermost tier, number 28062. Beside my wife and daughter … My consciousness drifts in a shallow sleep, my dream cortex linked to the complex's AI and interfaced with this drone. I am the eyes and ears of the project." My voice faded, became introspective. In a flurry I recalled the nightmares, filled with thoughts of a burning, angry desert, the decades drifting by with the sand on the wind, the lost race asleep amid the bones of perished nations. My metallic whisper trailed off and Cullaine shared a difficult glance with the Chinese woman, Chan. I pulled myself together. "Still, when this redoubt was built in the first years of this century, we were sure we were not alone. There are others in Russia, more in China, in Scandinavia and Japan, and probably elsewhere also. As millions fled into the sky, those who remained knew any hope of survival lay here, not in the vain dream of joining you Hi-Techers at L5." I slapped the railing below the windows. "This is the low-tech solution, and we have always believed it was the right one."

Zaitsin, my countryman, was unreservedly proud of all he saw. He was an engineer by trade, and appreciated the elegance of our solution. "A race in being—people of the late 21st century who will return and make the 23rd their own." He nodded with quiet satisfaction. "The continuity is amazing, and unexpected."

I nodded silently in return, but raised a cautioning finger. "Be warned, many resented those in the sky ... You ran away from the problems our ancestors caused, and left the rest of the human race to suffer the consequences." The silence was difficult, and I filled it with a coughing sound. "That was before all your times, I know. But not mine. Though your lives are much extended by technology, none of you was born before 2100, and The End. I have been *sleeping* since 2105. It is a sad reminder of the chaos of those last terrible years as the world became unable to support animal life, that your people and ours lost track of each other so thoroughly we now meet as strangers."

Cullaine checked the time display in the corner of her tablet and lay a hand on my arm, the human familiarity making my heart ache and underlining the loneliness I had endured. Her expression I recognized as compassion and in that moment I could believe it was genuine. "Anton ... We can't speak for those who built the cities in which we were born. But it is our mission and purpose to restore what was lost. The atmospheric balances you are monitoring are responding to *our* efforts. Do you not monitor the signal traffic between the space cities?"

"We have no means. We were ... unconcerned with the doings of those who turned their backs on us."

"Then let us show you something amazing," Cullaine said softly, gesturing to the world above and offering me her hand.

• • •

Evening thickened over the wastelands, a reddish sunset building through the dust, when we emerged on the surface. I looked up at the sky and stretched, the human expressing through the machine; if I could have wept I would have done so now, for never before had I left the redoubt. But my attention was drawn to the east, where clouds boiled in slow motion, and a shape beyond all reckoning lay at their heart.

"We call them Genesis Ships," Cullaine said, my hand still in hers. "This is the *Perun.*"

"Perun?" I returned in some small surprise, scanning the AI's database. "God of storms and head of the ancient Slavic pantheon."

"Just so. It was rather apt, we felt. In ancient times, storms were understood to be the harbingers of life. Nothing grows without water, and thunder and lightning are the bringers of rain, thus storm gods were often patron deities of agriculture. Each continent has its vessel. *Thor* works Europe, *Dian Mu* China, *Oya* cruises Africa, and *Mamaragan* Australia. The Americas are tended by *Thunderbird* and *Baka'b.*"

As we watched, a great fork of lightning played through the clouds and stroked the vessel, mirrored a moment later from another angle, then multiple strikes to the earth below the craft's oblate belly.

"The hull is charged," I observed in an awed whisper.

"The whole vessel is a lightning rod ... In her holds are

the systems that read DNA and write out proteins, turning raw materials into life. The seeds of the hardiest grasses, able to stabilize these sands, are made in that ship and scattered to the world below as she raises the storm. Each seeding run strips the moisture from the clouds, and makes the rivers run. A million storms have been triggered in the right places, a trillion-trillion seeds have rained from the clouds, and little by little, we are winning back Earth."

"However were they built?" I murmured.

"Each took around a year, much of them 3D printed. 1500 metres long, the largest craft ever to move on the face of this world. They were assembled by drones, much like yours. It took a decade to crack out enough helium to fill them, but time is one thing we have plenty of."

We stood in the last light of day to watch the behemoth creep westward, towing its vortex of cloud and fury, a marching curtain of blue-white strikes writing the furious command to life upon the desert. The rains came in concert, a silver-grey curtain that sent reaching fingers flooding through the dry bed of the Ural River on the slopes below us, and as the titanic craft made its stately passage I nodded my metal head, hands folded before me as my resentment, my apprehensions, melted away and I understood the scope of their achievement.

"The oceans, too, yes?"

"Each has its own vessel," Cullaine said softly. "Named for the sea gods, as you'd guess. They've spent fifteen years writing out the genes and proteins for phytoplankton and raining them into the spring seas. When their proliferation has raised the oxygen levels far enough, we'll introduce zooplankton. Then the first fish ... From the humblest building blocks of life, the great food web will be rebuilt ..."

"Now I understand," I said, raising my hands to the vista of the storm and the tremendous, organically curved vessel. "When we sealed ourselves into our redoubt we expected many hundreds of years to go by before natural processes began to repair the damage. A single century now seems more likely." A sudden elation gripped me, edged my voice with joy as the overwhelming image of the sunset-lit titan, wreathed in lightning, filled the sky before us. "Our own genebanks become merely a failsafe, a reserve. Ten years more and I will awaken our people. They will emerge upon steppes already green with a sea of deep grasses, the Kazakh desert driven south once more. We will rebuild Orenburg and see the first snows return in the highlands. The Ural shall flow once more, to swell and refresh the foul remnants of the Caspian Sea." I spoke with, more than passion, the sense of prayers being answered, and of gratitude for the revelation to have come upon me when faith was long since eroded by the grinding sameness of the decades.

"It's the dream of the age," Cullaine murmured against the near-continuous rumble of thunder, and we felt the first rain spots on our upturned faces. "It's good to think Earth was never quite as dead as we feared."

"Life persists," I returned quietly, and those two simple words were a summation of the will for Planet Earth to endure and overcome all we had, in our ignorance, inflicted upon it.

ABOUT THE AUTHOR

Mike Adamson holds a Doctoral degree from Flinders University of South Australia. After early aspirations in art and writing, Mike returned to study and secured qualifications in both marine biology and archaeology. Mike has been a university educator since 2006, has worked in the replication of convincing ancient fossils, is a passionate photographer, a master-level hobbyist, and a journalist for international magazines. Short fiction sales include to *The Strand, Little Blue Marble, Weird Tales, Abyss and Apex, Daily Science Fiction, Compelling Science Fiction* and *Nature Futures*. Mike has placed some 160 stories to date. You can catch up with his writing career at "The View From the Keyboard."

KANOHSA

Cathy Smith

TRICIA Hearst was in a good mood after a satisfying session of retail therapy. She'd found the gas mask she wanted to filter the air particles polluting the Metrodome. Her breathing was already improving, and she hoped it'd help her chronic cough. This success sweetened her mood so much she didn't mind checking out the mailbox.

Communications within the Metrodome were electronic. However, hard copies were used between the city-states. Her partner Rob had a Kanyen'kehà: ka penpal, Okwa: ri. Half the correspondence he sent to Rob was junk mail while the other times he sent care packages to them.

Tricia saw her reflection before she entered her home. She noted the beaded leather jacket Ohkwa: ri sent them the last time. It was hard to tell what pleased her the most about it. The fact it was so stylish or the fact it kept her warm. Though the gas mask she now wore marred the fashionable image she wanted to present.

Rob was looking at his terminal and screaming at the screen. "What's the use of living in a dome if they keep gouging us!"

Tricia rolled her eyes, "We're not moving out of the Metrodome to live in a tent city! Our life expectancy would decrease by decades."

"The Metrodome uses our fears to get cocky and overcharge us!" He called up the heating bill on a wall panel.

Tricia looked at the invoice. The numbers made her wince. "But our property taxes pay for heating!"

"Not anymore. Now they're separate. The property tax has stayed the same by the way."

"Bastards!" She was too tired to do more than sigh.

"Did Okwa: ri's letter come yet?"

She held up a properties for sale ad from Okwa: ri.

"Good! It's here!"

"Is he selling tipis?"

"His ancestors were into kanohsas, not tipis," Rob said.

The word "kanohsa" sparked Tricia's interest. "What is a kanohsa?"

On a nearby wall panel, Rob called up a scan he'd made from one of Okwa: ri's stills. It was a long rectangular glass dome with a rounded roof.

Tricia thought it must've been cleaned up digitally. No dome she knew of was that pristine or free from wear and tear. "How can that be a kanohsa? It's made of glass. I didn't think his people knew what glass was before First Contact."

"Kanohsas used to be wooden longhouses. Now they use glass and steel in the same design on a city-state-wide scale."

"They use? You make it sound like they still make new ones nowadays." She laughed but it started a coughing fit. She wouldn't put up with the abysmal air quality in the Metrodome if it were possible to move to a new dome.

"They do. The Kanyen'kehà: ka still have a union of ironworkers." Rob brought up a scan of living Kanyen'kehà: ka. They were in sturdy clothes with hard hats, thick, hard boots, and a full large leather belt full of tools.

"The Kanyen'kehà: ka ironworkers construct their domes themselves instead of using construction robots." Rob said. "The ironworkers passed their skills on throughout the last century."

"What are ironworkers?" Tricia sniffed.

"Before there were robots, construction work had to be done by humans. Even those big skyscrapers needed human workers to raise them."

Tricia gasped. "That doesn't sound safe! No wonder their work got automated."

"It wasn't, which is why it paid so well, even though it was blue collar work. The Kanyen'kehà: ka ironworkers were the last holdouts after robots got introduced as a safety measure. Now they're the only ones who do construction work. When the EMPs struck, the data outside the domes got corrupted. Yet the Kanyen'kehà: ka knew how to build, repair, and maintain domes without automated help. Their ironworker's union's gotten big. They're expanding from local work to taking on contracts outside their territory."

"Contracts?" Tricia frowned.

"Repairs, maintenance, expansions of old domes, and the construction of new domes. Okwa: ri offered to put me on the waiting list for housing in their model communities. I want to give Maurice an FYI, so he can inform the other council members."

Tricia sighed. "He'll say the ironworkers aren't needed. We've got automated systems." Though the malfunctions got worse every year.

"Which don't work as good as advertised. At the least we could use the ironworkers to 'expand our rafters.' Use them to create proper housing for the tent city outside our walls."

The mention of the tent city made Tricia bite her lip. Metrodome's tent city was the closest thing it had to suburbs. It was secured by a guarded fence with buildings that provided basic amenities. Refugees, immigrants, and those displaced from condemned sectors of the dome lived there. The tent city was the best that the Metrodome council could do for them.

"I'm only one vote on the council," Tricia pointed out. "You have to convince at least 100 more to get Maurice to move on your motion. There's no guarantee he'll be able to pull things the way you want it! Maurice will ask 'How do you know he didn't use a graphic arts program to forge the picture? A good one could pretty up a cracked dome or make a virtual one.'"

Rob answered by blowing up a tiny spot in the corner

that was the Better Business logo: their seal of approval. The picture was an accurate representation of the Kanyen'kehà: ka product. The datestamp was hard to duplicate and proved that the picture really showed a product for sale.

• • •

Tricia expected Rob to craft a cunning pitch, and he asked her to help him with the refreshments. She wasn't sure where she stood on renovation contracts. She tried to sleep on it but the nightly creaks from the dome's roof kept her awake. She was sure they had gotten louder since last year.

Tricia got out her mobile and did research on ironworking to use her insomnia constructively. She found papers on stress loads. They were full of jargon she couldn't understand. All she knew was that the dome's creaks alarmed her. The spate of quarantines made her wonder if her home district would be next. So far there hadn't been fatalities but the pieces of falling debris kept getting bigger.

She hated the almost annual rise in property taxes and fees in her district as much as everyone else. However, she thought of them as a necessary evil. These Kanyen'kehà: ka ironworkers were an option worth investigating. She could support Rob on this pitch, even if she wouldn't be surprised if Maurice turned it down.

• • •

"Do the Kanyen'kehà: ka have another cash crop venture?" Maurice asked as he sampled Rob's refreshments.

Rob had opened up their living room for the latest meeting to help establish the mood. "I'm presenting kanohsas, Maurice." The image of one formed on a wall panel. "These are being sold as prefabricated modules Kanyen'kehà: ka ironworkers assemble."

Maurice shook his head. "The council doesn't want to be liable for human construction workers."

"They produce quality work." Rob projected the results of various licensing bodies. They all passed the interdome certification board. "The ironworkers even have model communities."

Maurice closed his eyes. "Do you know how hard my family worked to move into the Metrodome to escape the Badlands? My father found work inside the dome. They put him on a ten-year waiting list before they found housing for him and his family. You expect me to want to move out after the sacrifices he made? The Metrodome isn't as good as it used to be but it's still the best thing around."

"We're being overcharged for basic amenities and overtaxed. Do you think we should let fear of change blind us to better alternatives?" Rob said.

"So, you actually want to do this?" Maurice asked.

"Yes, I want to check it out. If it's as good as I think it is, we should all move out of this unsafe structure."

Tricia winced.

• • •

"What are you doing with that thing?" Tricia pointed to a gun Rob had put into a holster on his left leg.

"It's mostly for hunting," Rob said.

"Mostly?" Tricia shuddered.

Rob shrugged. "It's also good for self-defense when you travel between city-states."

Tricia gasped at this. "I don't know you anymore!"

Rob shook his head. "I have to take this chance to see if there's anything better than the Metrodome. I want to see Okwa: ri's model community."

Tricia was convinced she'd never see Rob again after he finished packing. She didn't stop him, nor did she pack up her belongings herself. The Metrodome kept creaking at night.

The night before Rob would have gone, the creaking was the loudest it'd ever been. Then came a snap then a crash.

The alarm went off. Anyone who lived in the Metrodome recognized the code. This was an evacuation alert.

All of their home's lights came on. Their wall panels came alive. The words announced over the speakers scrolled on the panels. "This is not a drill. Everyone is to leave the area immediately. This is an emergency evacuation. This zone is now a red zone. Anyone who remains in the area does so at their own risk."

Tricia cried. "Everything we've worked for is gone. We're in a red zone now."

Rob took out her personal luggage. "The hotels and emergency housing will be crowded."

Tricia sobbed as she looked at the sight of the devastation on her mobile. "We'll be evacuated into the tent city."

Rob looked at her and held up his tickets for the timeshare demonstration he was travelling to attend. "We don't need to."

Tricia bit her lip and there was a moment of silence, then a ding from her mobile. Rob had discontinued his service to prepare for his upcoming journey. She was the only one who had contact with the council. "It's Maurice. The board called an emergency meeting. Bring your packet with you. They want you to tell them about the kanohsas."

"Okwa: ri can tell them himself. He's picking me up tomorrow."

• • •

Much to Trish's relief Okwa: ri came on time. She feared that he'd been running a long con on Rob. Though she counted on the kanohsas to solve their difficulties.

Okwa: ri had a rapt audience with the board. "I can show you a video of our open house." He took out a tablet and showed a recently datestamped tour of a model home. It was clean and had amenities.

"What's the neighbourhood like?" Maurice asked.

The video switched to a recording of the streets inside the kanohsa. They were empty but clean and in good repair with no signs of falling debris or fog from fine air particles.

"Let's go!" The people said.

• • •

When Okwa: ri came back with a convoy of vehicles and armed guards, Tricia was relieved. There would be safety in numbers. A large share of the people in the tent city were used to travelling in the Badlands and would follow them. The ones that didn't want to leave would take up residence in what was left of the Metrodome.

When the convoy approached their destination the kanohsa gleamed like a pretty bauble in the distance. Tricia sobbed when they made it past the gates into a model community with identical and new houses. There'd be enough houses for everyone in the Metrodome caravan.

Perhaps it was naive to expect perfection, but the kanohsa stood out like a beacon of civilization in a mad world. She was already breathing easier now that she was free from anxiety and the fine particles of pollution she'd been inhaling back in the Metrodome. She was already a satisfied customer of the Kanyen'kehà: ka and hoped she wouldn't be the last. The world needed their skills.

ABOUT THE AUTHOR

Cathy Smith is an aboriginal writer who lives on an Indian Reservation. She has also won an honourable mention from the L. Ron Hubbard's Writers of the Future contest and is a cowinner of the 2016 Imagining Indigenous Futurism Contest. You can follow her latest projects at
Wordpress: bit.ly/2e41qWT
Facebook: bit.ly/2dP3rXd
Twitter: @khiatons
Instagram: @cathy2891
Tumblr: bit.ly/2G3dEjo

BLEACHING EVENT

Lee Bell

As his wife passed through the hallway wearing a terrycloth bathrobe, her expression vacant, as if she'd slept in too long, Emery saw a painting through her neck. Her hair was up, the strands against her neck prematurely greyed, as was the rest of her, washed-out, losing substance. They hadn't had a decent conversation in weeks, not since moving to the beach house. He had thought the ocean air would do her some good, and he even bought her an expensive pair of running shoes so she could jog beside the tide with him. It would rejuvenate her.

When they were dating, Mira had warned him that she went through bouts of low moods. What he focused on was the word *bouts,* and the way she said it with a self-deprecating laugh that lifted her chin and showed the strong pillar of her throat. She twirled a straw around the melted murk of her margarita. He liked how easily she laughed then, how she could rattle off chemical concentrations in the atmosphere, and he liked the curling strands of hair against her neck, which were beginning to grey even then, in her early twenties. Now they were both nearing the end of that decade, and Mira had dropped out of her Environmental Science program. She'd never been able to finish her dissertation. Her running shoes still had the cardboard in them. Emery waited for this bout to be over the way he waited out a cough after bronchitis: impatiently, an ache lingering in his chest.

The painting filmed Mira's neck, a painting of the ocean, as if the cloud-scrawled view out the living room window wasn't enough. The ocean had to be inside, too, shadowing the hallway, shoring over Mira's skin. Mira went to the bathroom and after a few minutes she reemerged see-through, downright wispy. If Emery gripped her shoulders, his hands would pass straight through and meet somewhere in her chest, and the only thing he would feel would be his own palms. He watched her drift back into the bedroom where she would lie down in the bathrobe as if she had taken a shower and was waiting for her hair to dry, except she hadn't done either of those things.

He left. He took the car. He drove around town, drifting in his own way, though thank god more restless, thank god more burning, and crisp, and solid, *he* didn't let paintings show through his neck. He ended up at the only lively place in town, the brewery. Due to the tourists, the wait took an hour and when he was finally seated at the bar, the waiter mixed up his beer with someone else's order, a cider. The cider belonged to an older woman down the counter. He sipped her drink before realizing, then held the sip in his mouth guiltily, until the acidity pierced through the cold.

The woman scooted closer to exchange their drinks. He'd seen her before, around town, and at this same brewery. She shook off the mistake when he offered to buy her a new drink, smiling with chapped lips. She was friendly. He wasn't. She wore a heavy aviator coat that had a symbol of the aquarium on the arm, a wave that turned into an iconographic circle containing the aquarium's name. Its font was bubbles.

"I'm a volunteer," she said, seeing him look at the symbol. "I come here for lunch breaks. It's not the first time someone's drunk my cider. You from around here?"

"We've just moved here. My wife and I."

The woman's name was Frieda. She was happy to have young blood in town, and even happier to learn of Mira's studies in Environmental Science, which Emery reluctantly mentioned when he was waffling about revealing his wife's lack of occupation. Frieda said he and his wife should volunteer at the aquarium. Emery kept his face neutral. It wasn't quite tactless to solicit him as a volunteer. He stared into his glass, seeing his nose distorted in the brown liquid and thinking of his amorphous spouse awaiting him at the house.

"You take a few weeks of a class over the summer," Frieda was saying. "Then they assign you to one of the exhibits. I've been in the bird enclosure for five years. It's like getting to be a marine biologist and a voyeur at the same time! I could tell you so many stories about the mating pairs, especially the black oystercatchers." Frieda laughed, bunching in her coat like a puffin. She did look a little like a bird, rounded in a comfortable way but with a thin, keen face. After a moment she sobered. "Though it's a little sad to be a marine biologist right now. The poor coral. This year was one of the worst bleaching events on record."

"From El Niño," Emery cut in, feeling he ought to contribute something to the conversation.

"Not just El Niño," she said, scrunching her eyelids at him like a grandma who had caught him playing frisbee with a beached starfish. Mira used to joke that nobody killed the mood like an environmentalist. This joke usually came on the heels of her renewed fervour for composting, or pressuring him to eat a few days a week without meat, or swearing off grocery bags and straws.

When Emery managed a somber nod, Frieda turned cheerful again, and apologized saying, "You have a denier look about you." Then she said, "The thing about coral is," and from her shift in tone Emery knew he was about to learn a few things, and he pitied himself on his stool, which couldn't be discreetly edged away. "The thing about coral," said Frieda, "is that it has a symbiotic relationship with a microscopic algae, which feeds it and gives it those bright colours, all those nice reds and oranges. But if the ocean temperature rises, or there's too much pollution, the algae gets stressed and leaves, and the coral starves."

Emery knew all this. Emery had heard all this from his wife. The truth was, Emery hadn't noticed the painting before. The beach house had been a rental for tourists and it still had the old decorations with all their lackluster personality, meant to layer over the thoughts of the temporary occupants like frosting, flavourless and sweet, giving pleasure without the burden of nuance. Bland, peaceful oceans, as if peace needed to be diluted of any vibrancy to be effectively absorbed. He asked Frieda what he was supposed to do about the coral, convinced she would suggest something banal. Recycling. Watch your carbon footprint. Go running in the sand.

"Try scuba diving," was Frieda's reply. "Don't listen to me. See it for yourself first." She wrote the aquarium's number on the coaster. "Or come and volunteer with the black oystercatchers." She dropped the coaster into his lap. "You don't have to worry about them dying out. They live under a net."

At the beach house, Emery returned to find that his wife, resting in the bedroom, had made her full transformation to vapour. There was nothing left of her but a trailing fog across the bedspread, seeping into the seams. He would get her out of here, he assured her.

He took each corner of the bedspread and folded it around her. He carried her into the kitchen, and having not sworn off grocery bags, not completely, he put the bedspread inside of one, tying the ends together to keep her from filtering out while he transported her in the car, which he'd left running in the garage.

He put the bag on the front seat and untied it and waited for her to emerge from the folds of the bedspread. He told her he would drive her anywhere she liked. Just say the word. "A different beach," he said, knowing it would be the same beach, everywhere, with the same footprintless sand and the same bleached coral in the same painting on the same wall.

Mira started to coalesce, encouraged, he thought, by his voice. Maybe she'd just been asleep. His vison grew hazy. The car engine hummed its low carbon song. The ache spread through his chest and tremulously, watery fingered, crept over his mind and behind his eyes, where after a pass of dizziness he understood, he did understand, he thought, though he didn't really, he just wanted to—would that be enough?—and no sound of the garage door opening came to him until his neighbour was there, wrenching Emery's car door open the rest of the way.

"Don't do that," Emery said, but his wife had already dissolved into the damp air.

ABOUT THE AUTHOR

Currently an MFA student at Purdue, Lee Bell spends most of their time figuring out how to wrestle big feelings into small words, unpack the weird from the mundane, and face that horror lurking in the corner. Work also forthcoming in *Violent Vixens*, an anthology by Dark Peninsula Press.

OLD GROWTH
Steve Zisson

I was still procrastinating on my planned months-long process of cleaning out the office ahead of my retirement when old pal Roy Harvard interrupted with a call.

I didn't mind his intrusion. Most people clean out their office in a day, or in a few minutes if HR thugs are hovering over their shoulders. I'll be taking my time.

I gave into procrastination and took Roy's call.

"You've got to come see this," Roy said in his hyperbolic way. "I've found some old-growth forest!"

I removed a book from the shelf, put it into the empty cardboard box, and took a long breath. Progress. "I'm not up for another wild-goose chase, Roy. I'm packing it in. Where'd you find some now?"

"You'll never believe it. Right here."

"Right where?"

"Here. Massa-goddamn-chusetts!"

"There's no more old-growth forest here. You can't fool me into going on another hunt to nowhere. This is a ruse to get me to show up to a surprise retirement party. I told everyone: no parties. I just want to fade away into the woodland. Topple over and return to the soil."

He laughed. "There's no retirement party for a grumpy old state forester like you. Everyone's happy you're going. Especially your replacement. Get over yourself."

"OK," I trailed off, a little disappointed there'd be no party to not show up to.

"You've got to believe me. There's a hemlock off the Mohawk Trail that could be four or five hundred years old. We've got to get a core sample. You're the best at it even with your shaky hands. Bring that replacement of yours and see if we can find out what these old trees are saying to each other."

I thought about grabbing another book off the shelf. "Still don't buy it. This whole state has been clear-cut two times over. And now you just happened to discover an ancient hemlock somewhere in western Massachusetts."

"Yep. A local tipped me off to it."

Roy was getting up there too. Was it possible he'd simply lost it? I wondered whether he was just trying to relive the glory days of his big find of old-growth forest back outside Montreal in the '80s. The discovery that put him on the map.

Since this alleged old growth wasn't far away, I decided to humour him. One last opportunity to be in the field with my able replacement. Maybe she'd learn something too.

• • •

The next morning was as good a time as any to go on this quest. I drove the old pickup to our office parking lot to rendezvous with Naomi, the fungi whisperer.

She was leaning against her Tesla pickup when I pulled up in my clunky old junker. She looked up casually from her phone, pushed her short locs away from her eyes, and tossed her equipment in the back.

She hopped in the front seat. "Sure you don't want me to drive, Ted?"

"I'm not retired yet and you can't confiscate my license just because I'm so old. I'm not sure your pseudotruck thingy can handle the hills."

"Oh, it can handle. Have it your way. For a little longer."

She was just giving me the needle. I was comfortable with her as my replacement although sometimes I didn't let that on with her. I wanted to keep her on her toes so she could learn as much as possible before I left and faded into the forest, degrading into a pile of crumbly, spongy humus.

We drove in silence on Route 2 for the first fifteen minutes as she answered emails on her phone. It was early morning, too damn early to talk shop, and still cool enough that I could drive with the windows down. I like to drive that way to listen to the trees as much as I can with no traffic drowning them out.

Naomi came up for air from her emails and looked to each side of the road.

"Have you ever met Roy?" I asked.

"I caught the end of a panel he was on once."

"I've got to warn you he's old school."

"Older old school than you?"

We were falling into silence again when I thought I heard the trees talking to me. But Naomi beat me to it.

"Did you hear that?" she asked.

"I did."

"I didn't even have to use my equipment for that one."

"What did you hear?"

She rolled down her window and listened with a cupped ear. My old truck still has crank windows. For an old crank. "Not sure. Something something."

I leaned my head toward my open window. The trees around this area have gotten used to us. They know we can hear them speak through their mycorrhizal fungi networks. And they've found a way to broadcast to us without the use of Naomi's groundbreaking Natural Intelligence (N.I.) equipment. They've *learned* since she's been working with them.

This part of Route 2 doubles as the Mohawk Trail, which was once the main trading route for Native Americans between the Atlantic tribes and others in Upstate New York. I love it because it follows the Millers River and Deerfield River into the Hoosac Range where we're headed.

• • •

Before our silence overwhelmed us, we're in Florida. Not the state. Florida, Massachusetts, that is. We're at the Hoosac Range in the Berkshires. Lack of hikers in the area was probably why no one discovered this alleged old growth. If it existed or was all in Roy's mind.

Roy was waiting for us at the bottom of the hill. The hatch to his Subaru was open and he was sitting on the bumper, his legs crossed.

He stood as we approached.

"Finally," he declared. "I get to meet the great Naomi Jenkins, tree talker!"

Naomi let his rhetorical flourish whoosh past her and disappear into the mountain air. It was relatively cooler than in the valley on this August morning but the humidity was still brutal even here this early.

"She's great. But what about me?"

"You're ancient history," Roy said. "She's the future."

He was right.

Naomi hefted her backpack on in what seemed as noisy a manner as possible, grunting as she shifted the equipment inside to the middle of her back.

"Let's go old-timers. I'd love to lead but Roy, you're the only one who knows where it is."

"Allegedly," I grumbled.

Roy grabbed a walking stick out of his car and shut the hatch.

We found a gravel road at the far side of the parking lot. It was mostly flat at first then suddenly uphill.

"This service road is for the wind turbines and will take us to the top but we're only going about halfway until we dive into the forest," Roy said.

The young trees soon gave way to larger ones that hadn't

been disturbed in seventy-five years or more. Many of them were well over one hundred feet high but there was no hint of old-growth forest in them.

A half hour into our climb, we reached a hairpin turn. Roy shouted ahead to Naomi, "Here!"

She turned back to him. "Where?"

He pointed at a dense thicket. "This way," he said and took the lead, hacking at the brush with his walking stick.

Naomi followed him onto the narrow path that disappeared, swallowed up by greenery by the time I caught up. "Don't lose me!" I shouted through the branches scratching at my face.

A birch branch rebounded and smacked me in the ear. "Ow!"

No words of concern filtered back from the other two up ahead. I couldn't even hear them slashing through the underbrush anymore. I needed to catch up.

Running through the undergrowth, the branches slapping at my face, I stumbled into an open area and went down.

Naomi picked me up and Roy handed me my glasses.

"You good?" Naomi asked.

I was shaking but the forest floor duff layer had saved me.

"I'm OK. It was a soft landing," I said, stomping my feet. "This feels really healthy and very deep."

"Yeah. It may be the best duff layer I've ever seen," Naomi said. "I can't wait to get started."

With my glasses back on, I marvelled at one of the finest

examples of old-growth forest I'd ever stumbled upon or into.

Old-growth forest isn't a congregation of old trees confined to a nursing home, waiting to die. Old growth is the most vibrant and diverse forest ecosystem, with magnificent five-hundred-year-old trees, others fallen and rotting on the forest floor, seedlings, and a variety of smaller trees of numerous species stretching to the canopy among the towering old guard.

This was a hardwood upland forest of red and sugar maple, ash, beech, oaks. Yellow, black, and paper birches. Massive hickories, American chestnuts, and what we came to find, magnificent groves of ancient hemlocks. Towering above the others were stands of so-straight eastern white pine. And it was old growth and middle growth and young growth and all of the growth. The species were naturally spaced out so enough light made it down to the smaller trees, all growing together in a fertile soil of fungi and nutrients.

• • •

Naomi plunged her probe into the duff layer and her arm disappeared up to her shoulder beneath the oak and maple leaves and pine needles. She tried to pull it out but it seemed stuck as if something was sucking her down into the earth. Naomi grabbed her buried arm with her free hand and yanked. It finally gave in and popped out, covered in white strands of fungi, ants, and other crawly things and rich brown humus.

"This is wonderful," she said. "I just love the smell of

rotting things. It's very alive."

She placed her probe again a couple feet below the top layer. She turned to her laptop that was balanced on her backpack on the ground. With headphones, she listened.

"So much chatter. Amazing."

Roy leaned down and tried to pull one headphone off Naomi's ear but she waved him away. "What are they saying?"

"Quiet."

• • •

I assembled my increment borer, attaching the auger to the handle. Time to determine the age of this hemlock beauty.

Placing the bit at chest level, I twisted the core sampler into the huge hemlock. After several turns, Naomi flung off her headphones and covered her ears with her palms.

"They're screaming!" she yelled. "You're hurting them!"

I made a few more turns and stopped. It was probably all I needed.

Naomi was crying.

Roy and I helped her up. "Don't ever do that again," she said.

Holding out the core sample, I said, "What? I thought it didn't hurt them. How will we ever know their ages then?"

"The whole network of trees was in pain." She wiped her tears and looked around for her equipment before picking it up. "We'll know all about them because they'll tell us. With this." She shook her headphones at me.

I was sorry for all the pain I inflicted during my career taking core samples, these invasive biopsies.

Recovered, Naomi put the probe back in the hole in the duff layer.

"What are they saying now?" I asked.

She took off her headphones and said deadpan, "They're saying, 'We will outlast you.'"

I didn't know whether I was just so proud of these trees or frightened for humans. Either way, I was at peace. I fell backwards into the soft duff and did leaf angels, hoping this would be my final resting place.

This was their world and now Naomi's to tell us all about.

ABOUT THE AUTHOR

Steve Zisson is a biotech journalist whose speculative fiction has appeared in *Daily Science Fiction*, *Nature Futures*, *Brain Games*, *Selene Quarterly*, among other places. He edited a science fiction and fantasy anthology, *A Punk Rock Future*. He lives north of Boston.

THE CATS OF KRUGER

R. D. Harris

ASIA'S head rested in my lap as I ran her monthly diagnostics. Monthlies required a physical port for field-grade checks and she never failed to seize a snuggling opportunity.

The affectionate leader always came to me. Her brothers, Kivuli and Kisu, took their sweet time in wandering over for testing. Though all three cats were synthetic, they had their individual personalities that combined CPU programming with learning experiences.

"Messah," said Bandil, the supervising park ranger and my closest friend outside of Togo, over the radio, "will you soon be done with your diagnostics?"

"Soon, my friend," I replied.

"A poaching group is roaming the north zone. We need the cats."

I sighed. "Do you really need them? How many in the party?" The rangers tended to rely heavily on Asia and the boys. It was tough for me to see them as units like the rangers did.

"Three. Mercedes truck. I'll send the pictures when you give the green light."

"Very well."

Before the conversation ended, Kisu and Kivuli bounded over to me as they took playful swipes at each other.

I completed the monthlies and informed Bandil.

I stroked the leopards' furry heads. "Bandil's sending you an assignment shortly, guys." They comprehended most languages and I'd come to understand them and their individual behaviours. Asia had always been the leader. Kivuli, Mister Inquisitive, had mastered his stealth techniques while stubborn Kisu thought himself invincible. Even with slight drawbacks, the trio used their strengths to get the job done.

"Send the cavalry," said Bandil.

"You know what to do," I told the cats. "Go ahead."

Without hesitation, Asia sprinted into the distance with Kisu and Kivuli close behind. In seconds I could barely see them. Lanes of dust settled along their vacated routes.

I started my jeep and drove north.

With little training in self-defense or weaponry—being an engineer—I was often a distant observer during the apprehensions I actually got to witness. Even so, I enjoyed the infrequent thrills amid my worry for the leopards.

"Do you have eyes on the cats?" I asked Bandil.

"Through binos, yes," he replied. "They're assessing the situation, being cautious."

Minutes evolved to half an hour, with no further communication from Bandil or the other rangers. The north zone of Kruger National Park was eerily silent.

I radioed the rangers' encrypted frequency to reach someone. "Messah to patrol. Anyone out there?" Samuel, Yvette, and Paula would not, or could not, reply.

The jeep's headlights continued to burrow through the now-black trail. A near-infinite darkness supplemented by the sounds of nocturnal predators.

I nearly fell into a trance before gunfire startled me.

Jeep tires popped and the vehicle nearly rolled from my overcorrection. The left side of my conveyance crashed to the earth on its wheels after the close call.

While I sat stunned from the gunshots and the wreck, someone wrenched me from my seat and onto loose savannah dirt before floodlights blinded me.

I struggled to my feet, holding my right hip.

Bandil stood in front of me. Two women and a man, all three European, stood behind him. A fire was growing far in the distance behind the group. I looked at Bandil, confused.

"What're ... what's going on, Bandil? Where are the cats?"

"Distracted." Bandil nodded toward the arson. He trained his Sig Sauer pistol at my chest. My trusted coworker *had* been a dedicated ranger. I used to admire the native Namibian but now his smug smile fuelled an anger in me.

"The other rangers?"

His face was as stone. Samuel, Yvette, and Paula were dead. He offered an open hand to me. "The override."

Bandil couldn't control the leopards without it.

Four weapons pointed at me. My mouth was like cotton. I pulled the override pendant from my cargo pocket. It shook in my closed hand. A brief fantasy of pulling my gun, bagging the bad guys, and being a hero crossed my mind. No doubt they'd gun me down before my pea shooter left its holster.

"Give it to me, Messah." Bandil's voice and demeanour were calm, patient.

"Why not just kill me and take it?" I dared him to kill me. My voice shook through my defiance. "Did they not pay you enough?"

"You have your family at home. You have a lot to live for. That and we can't have the pendant damaged. I don't *want* to kill you so don't make me do it."

My arm moved to hand over the cruel device. What gain could I receive by yielding to his commands? Saving my own life? Self-preservation paled in comparison to the fate of Kruger's wildlife and the leopards created to protect them.

I placed the pendant back in my cargo pocket. "I can't." I stared him in the eyes. My tears welled. I knew the poachers would kill me. I hoped my wife and daughter would understand my principles and what was at stake. Martyrdom wasn't a desired end to life, but cowardice had no place in the Boukpeti lineage or among the Ewe people.

"I respect your decision and I'm honestly not surprised. Brave of you, Messah. Brave but foolish."

My long-time coworker raised his sidearm and stalled

with the muzzle near my forehead. I still believe he didn't want to kill me. However, he was beyond his personal point of no return. Too much money at stake for him to go back.

Bandil silently pleaded for me to give up the pendant, but a lithe shape knocked him from his feet. A crunching of bone soon followed.

Rifle rounds volleyed through the air. The poachers, panicked at the deadly blur they'd witnessed, shouted to each other in Dutch.

Exposed in the open during the chaos, I gathered my fight-or-flight senses. I ran for cover behind my jeep. But a round took me in the hamstring.

I cried out in pain. My college professors never mentioned being shot as an occupational hazard.

Asia slunk behind the jeep and nudged my wound with her nose. Rounds continued to go off as the poachers' truck engine started up.

"I think I'm OK," I told her, wincing.

The poachers fled.

"Where are Kivuli and Kisu?" The back of my leg felt as though someone had stuffed hot coals inside of it. Pain radiated around my thigh and into my knee. No doubt the bullet was lodged in my flesh.

In reply to my query, the synthetic cat stepped across me to look at the speeding truck. She calmly listened to wind-carried screams from the vehicle. Although it sounded like death throes, it was a simple, albeit messy, apprehension of the poachers. The cats had done their job—what they were made to do.

Asia sent a medical emergency signal for me and a call for auxiliary rangers to arrest the poachers.

Bandil lay contorted in an unnatural position. His lifeless eyes stargazed as if his spirit had escaped the trappings of money and temptation. I crawled over, straightened his body, and shut his eyelids.

Asia canted her head in curiosity as if thinking, *this man just tried to kill you.*

"He wasn't always bad." I took the override pendant from my pocket and inspected it. I didn't remember putting it back. "People are strange and complex creatures, Asia. You never know what we're capable of."

The drone of the fire response team's approaching medical vehicle echoed in the darkness.

Asia dug a shallow grave for the pendant. I followed her lead and threw it in before she covered it.

"We'll say it got lost," I told her. "We don't need it anyway."

To this day, I swear she was grinning.

ABOUT THE AUTHOR

Ryan grew up in North Carolina, but currently resides in Arizona. He served six years in the Marines as an administrative clerk. He loves time with his wife and kids, Spongebob Squarepants, 1990s action figures, and retro gaming. Let's face it, Ryan never really grew up.

Ryan's fiction has appeared in *Terraform[Motherboard]*, *Galaxy's Edge*, *Theme of Absence*, and now *Little Blue Marble*.

THE PRINCE OF SVALBARD: A SAGA OF THE THAW

Louis Evans

So. The Svalmen have always been renowned as the wisest and most warlike among men, and the most blessed. Did not the gods, in the frozen age before they made the world, visit Svalbard and there construct the great fortress Frøkvelv, and fill its catacombs and passageways with those seeds of wholesome grains that now grow both wild and cultivated across the land? Was not Frøkvelv wrought of godly stones and metals that hold fast against the weapons of any army? Did not they place upon the walls of Frøkvelv their protection, in magic runes that read, in the language of the gods:

SVALBARD GLOBAL SEED VAULT

And have not the gods been with the Svalmen since their first day, raising up heroes and warriors among them, men of renown on that land and on other lands across the great sea?

Know now the sad tale of the greatest and most defiled of these heroes, who strove mightily against the enemies of the gods and won much glory thereby, but in the end was ensnared in a demonic deception and brought to a base and tragic end: the tale of Ørretfangst, Prince of Frøkvelv.

Okred was king in those days, son of Gilesso, and when he was a young man he sailed and traded and raided all the lands around the land of Frøkvelv, and all agreed he was a strong man and a cunning one, and a fearsome foe in battle. And in the fullness of time he brought home a wife, a princess of the Easterlings, and with her he had a son.

Ørretfangst they named him, trout-trapper, after the fiercest beast of their land, which they knew by that name. The ørretfangst, mighty and clever, that waits hidden in stream or fjord for its prey and then strikes with a great clash of fangs, like spear on spear and shield on shield.

He was a strong lad, and grew up well, and was skilled with spear and sword and bow, and all men said he was the best of Frøkvelv in these things. And he learned well the catechism of the True Gods, who made the land and all the good things that man may eat, and who overthrew the tyranny of the Frost Giants, and brought the Thaw upon all the lands, and made the land of Frøkvelv a fit place for a man to live.

The seasons turned, and the prince became a man, and went out raiding. And he did many great deeds, both in raids and in defending the Kingdom of Frøkvelv, and all men said that he was a wise prince, and strong in battle, a worthy leader.

In the prince's sixth spring tilling the whale's road, he and his men went raiding upon the islands to the south of Svalbard. They raided that island that is called the sea's pipe, for its mountains are known to issue forth smoke. Thereafter they raided those islands that men call the Narrows, for so little of them remain above water. Before the Thaw, the seas were lower, and their waters were locked up in the vast palaces of the Frost Giants.

After the raids, when Ørretfangst was returning home to Frøkvelv, a mighty storm whipped itself up from the sea. Able seamen all were the prince and his men, and had they been otherwise their bones would have gone down to the bottom of the sea. But no man may bid a storm, and day by day and night by night the froth-tipped horses bore them onward.

When the sky cleared, Ørretfangst and his men found themselves near a strange coast. Ørretfangst, hawk-watchful, seabird-wise, had determined that the storm had borne them far to the south. Broddr, Ørretfangst's boon companion, said they should sail north at once, for men say that lands far to the south of Svalbard are hotter than may be endured, and have no natives, and nothing that is good for trading. But venturesome Ørretfangst, mighty of arm and strong of heart, would not be deterred by the words of men. Glory hungry, he sought to do great deeds heedless of reward. So they set their backs to rowing and brought their longboat ashore.

A strange land it was indeed. No man of Frøkvelv had stood in this place. Hot it was like an oven, a baking heat, and salty. The men removed their swordbelts and their loincloths and they tipped the longboat and sat beneath it, the burning sun low and watery in the south.

In the heat of the noonday sun they could not move about at all, but as the sky's coin sank in the west they organized scouting parties and set forth on this barren land in search of provender. Long they scouted and searched through that barren land, without reward. Not even weeds grew in this desolate place. But then they sighted the citadel of the gods, tall and proud upon the horizon.

As mighty as Frøkvelv rose the fortress, of god-stone and god-iron. Three great trunks it had, as the Easterlings' castle towers, but without any arrow slits or windows. From these large grey pillars issued a great roar. The fields around the fortress were sown with black glass, arrayed in rectangles and facing toward the sun.

"Armco, Ekson, and Ptro," breathed Ørretfangst, invoking three great chieftains from among the host of gods, their names foreign to his language but familiar to his tongue. Never had he expected to encounter another such marvel as the fortress of Frøkvelv.

Men gripped their spears and spoke words of fear, saying

that this thing was a work of the gods, who are fearsome to trespassers, or Frost Giants, who are worse. But Ørretfangst took not the counsel of cowardice, and he spoke to the men, saying:

"Before us we have a fortress of the gods! Mayhap men inhabit it, and mayhap gods, or giants. Mayhap it is abandoned, a haunt only for beasts and ghosts. I fear them none. I will enter the fortress and get its treasure: as gifts, as tomb plunder, or as war plunder. This I mean to do, and if I die in the doing, let my spear and shield be buried beside my bones in this alien land, so that all may say: here lies Ørretfangst, of true boasting and bravery."

Ørretfangst's brave plan and plain words rallied the men, and with spear in hand and sword within ready reach for every man, they set a march towards the god-wrought fortress.

Through the field of black glass they marched, and the march was easy, for they set their feet upon a godroad. Men find such roads, black-finished, long-weathered, in many places: wherever the gods had trafficked when they were making the world. Like all godroads, this was in disrepair; and its heat in the baking fires of the sun was a fearsome thing to behold. But a force of fighting men may march along a godroad at twice the speed they make along a path made by men, and so they came before the portal of the citadel of the gods.

It was no imposing thing, this portal, no high archway such as in the cathedrals that the richest kings of the faithful strive to erect. It was the height of a man, rectangular in shape, and wrought of metal.

Above the door there was an inscription in great runes of an unfamiliar type. Though Ørretfangst and Broddr were both skilled in runes, neither could read it. It looked like this:

LONDON CARBON SEQUESTRATION FACILITY 14G

Beside the door there was another inscription, in smaller runes, writ by hand. It had the appearance of a poem, composed of alliterating lines. The runes were these:

My house it lies under the ocean
My street it lies under the sea
Old London lies under the ocean
Oh bring back fair England to me

"Is it a curse?" asked Broddr, cautious-stepping, curse-fearing.

Ørretfangst, wise in witchcraft, examined the inscription and said it was not, and so fearlessly the men entered the great hall of the citadel.

And great it was. Once through the shabby portal, the fortress revealed its true splendor. Tall, it was, many times as tall as a man. The air was cool as in a cave, and the far reaches of the hall were invisible at that great distance. The walls were wrought not of wood, bone, hide, nor even stone, but of metal. Only the gods know the secret of forging the bones of a hall of any sort of metal. The walls of the place were not smooth or simple, as are the walls of the homes of the race of man. Instead, they erupted in a great profusion of made things, and were everywhere covered with peeling paint and other pigments, and half-preserved runic inscriptions.

Everywhere things were dark and silent, save for the low rumbling the Svalmen had discerned from outside. There was no immediate sign of human habitation, nor did they encounter any guard or watchman.

Broddr, whose name means the point of a spear, wished to rush forward with the party, seizing the fortress he now thought to be abandoned and plundering its goods. But Ørretfangst, clear-seeing, sure-thinking, bade him wait, and the prince of the Frøkvelvfolk turned his attention to the walls of the hall, and the arcane objects that protruded therefrom, which were made of iron.

When a man finds a godthing wrought of iron—an old signpost of the godroads, the bones of a godsteed, or a wrought thing more outlandish still—it is badly rusted, for the things the gods made were all made a long time ago.

But the iron bones of this hall were cleaned of rust. When Ørretfangst saw this, he knew that the citadel was not as abandoned as it seemed. Venturesome he was, yet also he was wise in the ways of ambush. Therefore he did not proceed into the dark hall, but instead struck his spear against one of the iron pipes, which rang like a war drum.

"Hark, strangers!" he called. "I am Ørretfangst, Prince of the Frøkvelvfolk and foremost among Svalmen! I have sworn to know this citadel, to serve its lord if he be pious and slay him if he be wicked, to receive gifts or claim plunder. Come forth and greet me!"

There was a long silence, as the mighty challenge echoed through the tall and narrow spaces of the citadel. And then with a strange clatter, witch-light blazed down from the ceiling. Bright and cold and grey it was, unwholesome and unwelcome. And the sound of footsteps began to echo against the walls.

Svalmen gripped spears closer and brought their shields to hand. Ørretfangst stood at their head, proud captain.

The sound of many feet became the sound of a single pair of feet, and then from a door in the side of the hall, the figure of a man came into view, and approached them.

As it approached the Svalmen could see it was no figure of a man at all, but a woman. And yet she seemed not as the women they knew. Her hair was short, her complexion peculiar. She was clad in an odd, sleeved robe, white and tattered.

"This is no lord or lady," said Broddr.

"Perhaps she is his thrall," said Ørretfangst. "In any case, she comes heralded by witch-light; her connection to the masters of this place is certain."

To the distant woman he pitched his voice, calling "Greetings, stranger!" using a man's courtesies.

The woman stopped some distance from the war party, beyond the reach of a spear. Her hands were at her hips. Beneath her cloak was a belt of leather and shirt and pants of linen. More clothes than Svalmen wear, either men or women. She bore neither spear nor shield, nor any other piercing or cutting weapon. Yet on her belt was a small thing of iron and wood, formed like the tiller of a ship, yet smaller, which the Svalmen did not recognize.

She spoke, then, a tongue that none of the war party knew, bland and strange. And then musically and swiftly in a different tongue.

"Speak you norsk?" asked Ørretfangst, for some foreigners know by that name the tongue of Frøkvelv, which is spoken on all the islands of the great sea, save for that mountain that men call the Fist.

"Ah," she said. "Yes. I talk norsk." Her tongue was slow-flowing, stutter-stopped, but with some speech and some gestures she was able to make her meaning known—and then work her foul magic.

"Who are you?" asked Ørretfangst. "Your land is unknown to us, your people unfamiliar."

"My name is Bridgid," she said. "I am the steward of this place, a learned woman."

"What manner of place is this?"

"It is a place for taking out of the air that which makes the world hot."

The Svalmen were aghast that anyone would work against the gods, who fought and defeated the Frost Giants, and more so that anyone would so readily confess to such evil purpose. Warlike words were spoken and warlike deeds contemplated.

"Hold fast," said Ørretfangst to his men, in the recondite tongue of the sagas, so that he would not be understood by a woman so unfamiliar with norsk. "Barbarians and foreigners have strange practices and foolish beliefs; perhaps this woman is simply confused."

To the woman he turned once again, saying, "Explain to us this work of yours. Why do you do it?"

And then she wove about the prince the deadly snare of the Frost Giants, the terrible lie that overthrew the reason of the greatest prince Frøkvelv had ever known.

"In the days before the Burning," she said, for it was by this name and this name alone that she referred to the Miracle of the Thaw, "the race of man was numerous upon the world. The world itself was temperate and plentiful, and many hundreds, hundreds, hundreds—" she seemed unsatisfied with such numbers as she could describe to the prince and his band—"countless more men were alive than are now."

The men laughed at her, saying, "This is nonsense! For when it is warm, the crops grow tall and plentiful, and when it is cold, they fail, and many a mother's son goes hungry." But the prince did not laugh; he regarded the thrall of the Frost Giants calculatingly. Already her sorcery had begun to work upon him.

"There are lands to the south," she said. "Great lands, where a man may ride the fastest steed for a month and still not reach the ocean. Once they were peopled; now they are barren, as even this land is barren."

This impressed the men little, for a seafarer knows there are always more lands beyond the sea's bright peaks.

"So much of the earth is not as it was, for men burnt the whale-oil of the ground, and the tinder of rock, and these fires sent up an unwholesome fume into the sky, and made the climate much hotter than it was formerly."

"You are incorrect, lady," said Ørretfangst. "For all men know it was the gods who made the world warm, as it is today."

"I tell you it was men! And we, all of us across many lands, seek to return the earth to her erstwhile condition, with green growing things to the far south, and land where there is now sea, and yea, ice at the poles."

"So you admit you are about the work of the Frost Giants," cried Broddr, the prince's bosom companion and soul mate.

"There are no gods or giants!" said the thrall. "Just men, and their folly, and those who would repair—"

But at that instant Broddr became so enraged by the thrall's blasphemy that he struck her in the stomach with his spear, seeking to kill her.

It was a strong blow and the spear ran her clean through the belly. But it was not her deathblow, and she reached down to her belt and raised up that object that the war party had not recognized, which was neither spear nor sword nor bow.

But in that instant they knew it to be a thunder-spear, that weapon of the gods and giants. For when she brandished it there was a noise like thunder, and Broddr fell dead, face slathered in blood. Again she brandished the weapon and again the noise like thunder, but Ørretfangst seized her about the throat and snapped her neck, and that was the end of her days.

Ørretfangst claimed the thunder-spear as a trophy, and the men of the war party coursed through the great hall and the many narrow passages of the fortress of the Frost Giants, seeking plunder and giantish foes.

No giants were there, but much plunder of good godstuff: wire for bracelets and armbands, and glass for necklaces and ornaments, a waterskin of godmetal, and a quantity of gold, which they found in strange chests, affixed to green wafers in obscure patterns. Books of sorcery they found, and with them they made a pyre and burnt Broddr, for one who is felled by a Frost Giant's weapon requires a funeral of burning to purge the cold from his soul. And the spare volumes they burnt for warmth, and to toast meat. The thrall's foodstore they found, and paltry and strange though it was, her bread and curds sustained them.

During the plundering the groaning and growling of the great fortress fell silent, and the men were relieved, saying that the ill purpose of the Frost Giants had been well thwarted.

After the passage of days there was no more to plunder in that mighty keep, and so the men retreated to the boat along the ruined godroad, so laden with treasures that they did not even stop to pillage the wide fields of black glass that surrounded the citadel.

On the godroad they made good time to the boat, which they set aright and launched to sea at once. And with good seamanship and a good wind they returned safely home to the land of the Svalmen, to the great fortress of Frøkvelv. But men who were there said that Prince Ørretfangst was in a strange humour indeed, silent and contemplative, not taking his ease with his fellows nor sharing their counsel.

Now, the fortress of Frøkvelv is the work of the gods, and no structure made by man can match it. And yet the city of Frøkvelv is also the greatest city of man in this age. Its walls are hewn of stone and rise twice again as tall as the tallest man, and within it are many buildings of wood, and of those buildings more than half a dozen of them are of two stories. But when Ørretfangst's gaze fell upon the city of Frøkvelv it was not with awe, but with lordly disdain and sorrow. And men looked upon him and said that something ill had come into his heart.

When the war party landed, Prince Ørretfangst betook himself to the hall of his father, King Okred, and his troop followed faithfully, though the wisest among them had a sense of grave foreboding.

In the hall of the king, Ørretfangst stood before all and recounted the events of his journey: of the storm that had blown him from his course; of the barren land to the south; of the fortress of the Frost Giants and of the woman-thrall; of the death of Broddr and his burning; of the good plunder brought back to Frøkvelv.

When King Okred heard the tidings of these events, he

knew his son and his son's fighting men had acquitted themselves bravely, and he praised them, and gave them many gifts, and swore to uphold their names and always be a true friend to them.

But when Ørretfangst explained the workings of the Frost Giants and their thralls, the king grew gravely concerned.

"Then this is no simple raid nor feud-killing," said the king. "It is the occasion for holy war."

The king spoke to the assembled war band, and all of his retainers, saying, "With the strength of the gods behind our right arm, there is no scheme of the Frost Giants we cannot overcome, no citadel of theirs we cannot storm and take as plunder. I therefore beseech you, Ørretfangst, if this cause seems good and righteous, to take up your followers and your ships, and sail southward, and seek out the other citadels and seize them by force of arms, and slay their thralls and end their wickedness."

And all who were present were sure that Prince Ørretfangst would do this thing, for he was boldest among men, and known for boasting, and better yet for doing the deed boasted of.

"This thing I will not do," said Ørretfangst.

"That is ill said," said the king, and all the men of the room drew closer to their swords, for when a king and a prince quarrel, much blood is shed.

"He speaks manliest who speaks the truth," said Ørretfangst. "I claimed the thunder-spear as a trophy of battle, and on the long nights of the journey I contemplated its riddle. For this thunder-spear was not made in the time of the gods! Its grip is wood, and new wood at that; I have looked into the grain. Nor was it as well made as the thunder-spears of the gods, for they were made all of godmetal, and could slay many men in an instant.

"But if this thunder-spear was made after the time of the gods, and with the materials of man, then it was made by man. And if the thrall, whom we slew, made this thing or was given it by the man who made it, then she knew much of men and gods and giants that we do not.

"And in the thrall's rooms there were many maps," said Ørretfangst, and at this time he took out from his tunic these parchments, which he had kept in secret. "They bear out her tale! Behold the vast lands to the south!"

The king's face was grim and cold. "So far you have said many things, Ørretfangst. But what would you have done?"

"We should sail south, yes. We should seek out another fortress and treat with its master. We should pay the death-price for the one whom we killed, and do great feats in defense of these places, and when the seas fall, we should claim all the new lands of Earth for the kingdom of Frøkvelv!"

And then the king's face was terrible, not with anger but with sorrow.

"I see now that the Frost Giants' witch has snared your wits," he said. "It is a venturesome dream you have, my son, but it is a madness and a heresy." And men nodded, for they saw that the king was right.

"No!" cried Ørretfangst, his face deranged with his madness.

"Seize the prince," said the king, "and put him in shackles, that he may not strike out in his madness and slay, for he is still the strongest and most warlike of men."

And it was done as the king commanded.

For six months they kept the prince in shackles, and the doctors and sages of Frøkvelv sought desperately to treat his madness. But the sorcery could not be broken, and Ørretfangst's ravings grew only more mad, until he denied the gods and giants, and gave voice to the heresy the woman in white had espoused.

Men said he should be burned as a heretic, and given back to the god Ekson, scourge of the blasphemer, whose other name is Mobil. But one night he slipped his bounds and escaped into the swamps. Many men searched for him, and a close watch was kept over the boats, lest he attempt to make good his mad quest. But no man at arms of Frøkvelv could find the prince, then or after.

Meanwhile the king was as good as his plan. That spring, and each spring since, when the storms abate and the land may still be crossed without heat sickness, the bravest of the men of Frøkvelv take up the spear, the sword, the shield, and they sail south, guided by the thrall's map, and they seek out the Frost Giants' citadels. And the Frøkvelvmen put the thralls within to the sword, and pillage the citadels, and lay to waste the machines and workings of the Frost Giants. And so it is that the men of Frøkvelv do what they can to hold back the coming of the second age of frost.

Yet winter upon winter grows colder, and now men go about wrapped in skins from head to toe during the longest nights. And those venturesome men who sail north into the darkness, under the gem-cloth of the gods, report that strange new storms may be found in these waters, like unto neither rain nor hail, but instead of the smallest stinging flakes of bitterest cold, which burn the skin and bring unnatural pains unto the flesh.

And to this day, men on journeys through the marshes and bayous that separate Frøkvelv from the other settlements still sometimes see mad Prince Ørretfangst, an outcast and an outlaw, a wild man with beard and clothes in tatters, living like a beast amongst his namesakes, the ørretfangsts, the crocodiles of Svalbard.

ABOUT THE AUTHOR

So. Louis Evans has always been renowned as the wisest and most warlike among writers. Long have his songs been sung, in *Nature: Futures*, *Analog SF&F*, *Interzone*, and more. In spider's weft his hearth is evanslouis.com; on birdsong he is heard @louisevanswrite.

A CHILD GAMBLES IN PETROLEUM COUNTRY

Deb O'Rourke

THE indigo amphora of night slowly fills with light.

Its sapphire body dawns through cobalt,
to lapis, before the sky flattens into an azure
plate that the sparrows crawl on like ants.

My favorite marble had the depth of predawn
sky, from oceanic core to atmospheric edge
of teal. The size of my eye, brought near,
trails of tiny bubbles were revealed—yet
smaller universes spun within its cool vista.

We children gambled with our marbles:
Cats-eyes,   irised yellow and red,   chased
one   another   through
                  the   asphalt   schoolyard.

"Crystals" were the special prizes: clear like an ice
sphere, green or blue like a planet, a rare garnet red.
They would be the last out of a pocket and   gone.

I never played my blue marble, only took it out
to look—instant azure joy.

But as gamblers do, we played until all were
cleaned out. All except for the bullies who could end
any game by shouting, pockets full, and storming away.

One day, my eyes told them I held back. So
"Play it, play it!" they yelled

                    ... .

Thus was   my blue marble

lost
        in a concrete and gravel   schoolyard   game.

ABOUT THE AUTHOR

Deb O'Rourke's prose appears in various cultural and journalistic publications, most notably in Toronto's weekly, *NOW Magazine*. Her visual art can be seen at milkweedpatch.com. Some of her work in democratic education is documented at michaelbarker.ca. Her poetry has appeared in the Banister and William Henry Drummond Contest anthologies, and placed second in *The New Quarterly*'s Occasional Poetry contest in 2016 and 2019. Born in Alberta of Canadian settler descent, she lives in Toronto.

FARMERS

Arlen Feldman

BHOLA, Bangladesh, 2033

Nayeem Abedin dumped out food for the geese and chickens. They dove for the food hungrily, oblivious to the rain.

Nayeem, dressed in a short-sleeved khaki shirt and a tube-like lungi around his waist and legs, was not quite so immune to the downpour, but he had work to do, so he did it. Every now and then, though, he looked up, then looked worriedly towards the rice paddies. It had been raining continuously for eight days now. The rice needed to be in water, but if the seedlings disappeared completely below the surface, they wouldn't be able to breathe.

It was OK so far, but another day or two of this, and they'd be in trouble. There were still more seedlings to transplant into the paddies, and they could rescue more from the existing paddies if they started soon, but they'd need expensive insecticide. The government was trying to encourage use of even *more* expensive natural insecticides, an impossible outlay for Nayeem this year.

It was also going to be harder with only three of them—him, his wife, and youngest son, Tasfin. The other two sons had both moved to the city hoping to work in Bangladesh's burgeoning tech field. A frown crossed Nayeem's face, but quickly disappeared. His dark face, with its thick, bushy mustache, was timeless. A stranger might think he was thirty or sixty, although he was actually only forty-one.

He'd been a farmer all his life, from a long line of farmers, and he had no interest in the city. Maybe he had when he was younger. Maybe, he thought, his sons would get their fill and come back. Maybe he'd better get back to work.

• • •

South Dakota, United States, 2033

Standing beneath the ancient bur oak, Josh watched his father's truck come up the road, a plume of dust rising behind it in the heat haze. The dirt road went straight as an arrow between fields of wheat, the stalks all around two feet tall, softly waving in the wind as far as the eye could see. Wheat was their standard summer crop, although this summer was a little bit too warm. It might reduce yield a little, but not too much—twenty years of experience let him judge the crop by eye, and by chewing on a few sample kernels.

While Josh was musing, the truck pulled up, and his father got out. The lines on Robert Merton's face attested to his more than sixty years, but his wiry body still stood ramrod straight. He had on jeans and a checkered shirt over a white T-shirt—the same outfit that Josh was wearing, except for the shirt pattern. Unlike Josh, he wore a baseball cap with a faded John Deere logo. Beneath its brim, he looked worried.

"Peterson's gone," Robert said

"Peterson's an idiot," replied Josh.

Robert thought about this for a while. He generally thought before he spoke. "Yeah, maybe. But he was paying same as us for water."

"Not really, Pops. We locked in the price six months ago. Peterson was convinced that prices were going to drop, and he left it too late. We're good for this year."

"And next year?"

When did our roles reverse? Josh wondered. He remembered his father always having the answers, always knowing what to do. Now worry shrouded his father's eyes. His father was a farmer, not an accountant, not an engineer. He knew everything about crops, but nothing about the way the world worked now. If Josh hadn't stayed on the farm, the farm couldn't possibly have survived.

Josh smiled at his father. He had his own worries, but the big one, right now, was to reassure his father.

"Well, I think I have that handled, too. The pivot system is too wasteful. I want to switch to a drip system. It's expensive, but I've applied for a grant. There's also a big tax break."

Again, the long wait, but Robert was obviously relieved— less about the specific plan, than about the fact that there *was* a plan, Josh suspected. "Didn't know you could get grants for that sort of thing."

"Sure, if you're willing to wade through the paperwork. There's lots of funding out there for cutting down on water usage. It's just a matter of finding it."

Which had taken him about two months, but he didn't bother pointing that out. As conditions had worsened, there were a lot more programs coming into being, but it was all a disorganized mess. Actually, that was probably an advantage—if it were easier, there'd be a lot more competition.

"We won't be able to do the whole 300 acres in one year, but we'll get a start. Assuming everything goes according to plan, we'll be ready after the soybeans, before the corn, next year."

This led to a discussion on seeds, yields, and weather, and then into politics and then sports. After about twenty minutes, the conversation drifted to a close. Robert put his hand on Josh's shoulder, which, for the old man, was about as emotional as he got. Josh had always sworn that, with his own son, he would be more demonstrative with his feelings but, really, looking at his father's face, feeling the pressure on his shoulder, he realized that his father was saying everything that needed to be said.

After a moment, his father turned and got back into his truck, and Josh watched the truck disappear before he climbed into his own Ford F-450 and headed in the opposite direction.

• • •

Bhola, Bangladesh, 2038

Nayeem was not at the farm when the storm hit. His eldest son Sayeed had called him two days earlier, and Nayeem, his wife, and Tasfin had crammed into Sayeed's apartment in Dhaka, along with Sayeed's wife and two young children.

They had been practically glued to the images on Sayeed's flat-screen TV, drinking endless cups of hot sweet tea. Even in a country used to storms, Cyclone Nilam was huge, with winds of 350 kph. It was being compared to the 1970 storm that killed over half a million people, but it looked to be much worse.

After the storm was over, Sayeed drove them back to the farm. He'd wanted to wait longer for the roads to be cleared, but Nayeem had insisted. It had taken days, and they finally only knew that they'd arrived because of the GPS on Sayeed's phone.

Nayeem got out of the car and looked around. At first, it looked as though God had taken an eraser to the whole landscape. The waters had receded, but it took several minutes for Nayeem to find any landmarks he recognized—a hill that marked the boundary of his property, remnants of an old fence, the ragged remains of a shed. As for their bungalow, the cyclone had reduced it to a few random sticks.

His wife Alina came up next to him and put her arm around him. She said nothing, but she shook against his side. Then she pointed. A chicken. Then several chickens, waddling towards them, hoping to be fed. Allah, he decided, had kept them alive as a sign.

Tasfin looked at his father, waiting for some sort of guidance.

"Let's get to work," he said.

• • •

South Dakota, United States, 2038

Josh stood in his favourite spot, beneath the bur oak, looking over the fields. Something about watching the golden wheat waving slowly in the wind eased away some of his cares from the day. Wheat was now their prime winter crop, covering 200 acres. They'd switched to drip irrigation earlier than most, and it had saved them when a lot of the other local farmers were literally being dried out from their farms—some of them going back generations.

Now, of course, things were different. The government was handing over money, and providing "experts" to every farmer who would stand still long enough. In a few months, Josh would plant genetically modified corn that required twenty percent less water. Also, for the first time, they were going to start growing beans—a good low-water crop.

In a funny way, the conditions over the last few years had been really good for the remaining farmers. Prices were up and, even with price controls, his family would make a bigger profit from the smaller crop that they could produce within their water allotment. Still, the farmer in him hated leaving so much land fallow. He knew that it was worse for his father. Embracing change had not been easy for the old man, although Josh knew he tried hard to not show it.

Speaking of his father, Josh was going to be late meeting him for dinner. He climbed back on his dirt bike—they only used the trucks now when truly needed, to save money—and headed back to the house.

•••

Bhola, Bangladesh, 2043

Nayeem and two of his sons worked quickly, cutting the stalks with sharp curved knives, and then carrying bundles to the gas-powered thresher, leased along with its operator. A dozen other men worked alongside them—representatives of a massive new class of men who'd previously had their own land, but now worked as cheap labourers whenever they could.

Sayeed was still working in the city, making a good living now, but Hasan, Nayeem's middle son, only worked sporadically, and still came out to help on the farm.

They'd lost the first harvest this year to flooding, but this crop looked good, and hopefully they'd get in a third without trouble. This new, hardier breed of rice—provided by an NGO—grew taller, faster, and didn't require insecticide, although it also had a lower yield. Part of the bargain for getting the new rice was keeping the sell price the same as for the classic aus rice they'd previously grown, so profit would be smaller too. Truth was, Nayeem didn't worry about it, just losing himself in the rhythmic patterns of the work, letting his mind go blank.

In his more introspective moments, Nayeem thought about the fact that he was part of a tradition reaching back thousands of years. Some good years and some bad years. Lately, there had been a lot of bad years, but that was just what fate had decreed. He hoped that his sons would have better years, but either way, they would take their place in the long chain.

• • •

South Dakota, United States, 2043

It had been two years since his father's death, but Josh was thinking about him now. His own son, fourteen years old, was standing next to him, underneath the old bur oak.

Robert had died of malaria of all things, which seemed crazy in South Dakota of all places, but for a while had been a serious problem. Now, everyone had been vaccinated, but it didn't make the mosquitos any easier to bear.

Josh looked down at his son, but at the rate that he was growing, he'd soon be looking him in the eye. Blond-haired and good-natured, Rick Merton seemed to have inherited the love of the land from his father and grandfather.

Josh wanted to say something to him, let him know how proud he was. Let him know that, however hard it got, good years, bad years, lost crops, changes—always changes—they would find a way through. Somehow, though, the words would not come. Instead, Josh reached over and squeezed Rick's shoulder.

ABOUT THE AUTHOR

As well as writing fiction, Arlen Feldman is a software engineer, entrepreneur, maker, and computer book author—useful if you are in the market for some industrial-strength door stops. Some recent stories of his appear in the anthologies *The Chorochronos Archives* and *Particular Passages,* and in *On The Premises* magazine, with several more coming out soon. His website is cowthulu.com

REPLANTING THE GARDEN

Liam Burke

THE airborne drop ship Yggdrasil, TREE class vessel, soared through the clouds of gathering CO_2, claxons blaring a warning that go time had arrived. Each Planter's indicator light flashed green in a blinking series of eagerness. Every bioengineered drop pod's fully formed payload was ready to be fired directly into the soil of the Houston Ruination Zone. It was a forest given wings, a true World Tree within the Terrestrial Restoration Environmental Engine ship.

T-minus six minutes to launch, the onboard AI informed the crew, who interfaced with the ship and madly ran through the prep protocols for Planter expulsion. Abosede Ethreaf and the two other Gardeners jogged down the length of the hold, envirosuits growing out from the implant seeds in their chests.

The pace of the Gardeners' motion built as the suits enveloped them, boosted by the blood slamming through their hearts and galloping through their veins. Lighter brown membrane covered Abosede's midnight dark skin inch by rushing inch. Phil's caramel complexion and Unnulf's alabaster white disappeared under the same bark tones.

"Dropping in five, boys. Ready to save the fucking planet again?" Abosede called out as the final stage of her esuit subverted, then enhanced her senses. Fully cocooned, she sprinted with the rush of strength and weightlessness that came with the trickle of growth serum, Planters and crew blurring past. She revelled in it, the creeping slowness of aging forgotten.

"Here's hoping it all goes down like clockwork," Phil answered to her left. Volatile organic chemicals echoed his thoughts through the esuit's connection to her mind, along with Yggdrasil's VOCs in the background.

Both he and Unnulf kept pace with her easily, their own enhanced states making sprinting feel like a casual stroll.

"It won't, and you know it. That is what they are having us for," Unnulf chided, his practicality igniting hope in Abosede's chest. She lived for this shit, and wouldn't know what to do otherwise. Their population was too low for slackers.

Suits fully grown, the group slid to a halt, small roots at their feet joining with the bark of the inner hull's mesophyll. Next to them a smaller pod, elephant sized instead of a gargantuan Planter, opened like the maw of a Venus flytrap.

Inside sprouted the Garden Tools, provided by WEPAN, the World Environmental Protection Agency of Naturalization. The team geared up, the AI chiming the two-minute mark. Unnulf took his massive Gatling gun and spear, Phillip his arm-encasing hand cannon and repair-kit seed. Abosede hefted her signature pair of SMGs and curved sword. All stunning grade.

"Hell yeah," she murmured, and the other two chuckled.

"What're you up to, Abosede? Ten, twenty years Gardening?" Phil asked playfully.

She shrugged, her contented wistfulness conveyed on the VOC. "Time flies when you love what you do. Do you think about it?"

Unnulf stoically replied, "We contribute, that is enough."

Phil snorted.

Abosede twirled and holstered her armaments. Her esuit grew around the weapons, fusing them to her body. "I hope so. It's time. The Planters are launching."

Assent channelled across their link, and they switched to interface with Yggdrasil directly, seeing with the senses of a flying titan.

Abosede's worldview exploded, the taste and texture of light waves bombarding her as the TREE ship gazed down at the shattered world below. Shades, pigments, the *direction* of the sun's rays painted a picture screaming in hues most people never knew.

The ship expelled the Planters, spitting them out of the organic hull and hurling them to the broken forest line.

Seventeen tremendous hybrid arboreal columns pierced soil, containers exploding out as the overload of growth serum caused roots to aggressively grasp the world. Trunks soared and leaves materialized, pumping out gouts of oxygen.

All but one.

The Planter skidded on the surface, furrowing the street and sidewalk it was meant to impale, trajectory terminating with it skewed and jutting up like a hangnail of failure. Yggdrasil's voice wailed in their blood at the sight.

Planter 672 has failed. Insufficient carbon reduction imminent. Recalculation of weather patterns indicates reforestation will be required in Jacksonville Fissure. Success reduced to suboptimal levels. Window is fifteen minutes.

"Oh no," Phil muttered.

"As was expected," Unnulf mused.

"Oh hell yeah!" Abosede pushed the TREE back into her subconscious.

"Isn't that a major rokkoon breeding zone?" Phil reminded them, and Abosede's good mood shifted.

"Shit. It is." She'd planned on making one of the bison-sized raccoons—her favourite mutants—a pet someday. If they didn't settle the CO_2 levels here, she'd never get that chance. "All the more reason to get that Planter fixed. Gardeners, prepare to deploy!"

Her mind sank into the ship again, instructing it to expel the three Gardeners, miniature projectiles to suture the wound below.

"Keep it tight, do no lasting harm. And above all else?"

she intoned.

"*Leave it better than we found it!*" her team replied, as the ship snatched them, spun them, and spat them at ridiculous speeds to the wasteland below.

Unnulf and Phil exchanged chemical glances of unease as they fell, Unnulf broaching the difficult subject across their link.

"Are you sure you are up to this, Abosede? In training your reflex time—"

"Was passing, and then some." She struggled to keep her doubt and frustration from them.

"Aye aye, team lead." Phil politely hid his misgivings.

Abosede grunted, a cloud of spores conveying her annoyance as she refocused.

Seconds before they crashed to their certain deaths, their suits sprung sweeping leaves, grown in milliseconds and halting their fall. WEPAN provided the best. Humanity had learned through pain not to cut corners.

Instead, each Gardener landed, crouching and drawing weapons to deal with the onslaught of rokkoons. Slavering, frenzied from fear as the earth rippled and shifted around them, the mutants screamed and attacked whatever was nearest.

The Gardeners, ranged armaments whirring, stunned beast after beast from every direction, roots from the expanding trees churning the ground around them. Smaller tubers on their esuits' feet let them keep their balance as they fought their way to the lopsided Planter.

A furry maelstrom reared up by Unnulf, who dropped his oversized autocannon. A vine deployed from his back caught the weapon as he drew his spear and stabbed, the stun function shrieking to life with enough power to drop the creature and send it flying six feet back.

Abosede's focus shifted rapidly between targets, and she lost herself in the thrill of combat, knowing it was all fun and games since no one would even lose an eye. Idly, she sized up the rokkoons, debating which one she might take home and cuddle.

The team finally reached the tilted tree, Phil's repair seed ready. Occasional blasts from his direction let them know he hadn't been unmolested, only a slight failure on their part.

As the other two battled, Phil slammed his apparatus down into the ground. As he integrated with it, his instructions echoed in the back of Abosede's VOC connection. Branches leapt forth, connecting with the Planter, slowly righting it.

"It's fighting me!" Phil shouted. "We have to bail, there's too many!"

Ten-minute window in this region, Yggdrasil sang in their veins.

Unnulf grunted, clusters of screeching animals falling comatose before him. Abosede drew her blunted stunning sword, quarters too close to aim a projectile weapon. She ignored the weariness in her arms, her esuit mitigating the lactic-acid buildup.

These animals would die if the Gardeners left. She made

the call.

"Keep going!"

A rokkoon lunged for Unnulf from his blind spot. Abosede leapt, sending warnings silently along their network. She landed too late. The mutant sank teeth into Unnulf's side and dragged him out of sight.

"Unnulf!" she cried. Phil paused, the Planter nearly in position. He looked at her, questioning.

"Do not stop, I will get him back!"

Phil nodded, commanding the seed to surround him in a protective shell, peach-pit hard. It would last, but not long.

Abosede dashed after Unnulf's weakening signal. Her legs like lead, she had no choice but to increase the growth serum from her esuit and risk mutation. Fatigue sloughed off, and she ran with the rokkoons, occasionally swatting especially aggressive bulls. Unnulf would *not* pay the ultimate price for her decision to stay, for her aging reflexes.

Eight-minute window.

The swarm led her to an old Houston building, an office complex, Yggdrasil explained. Abosede smashed through walls, esuit allowing her to ignore cement and drywall alike. Nature they would preserve, the old ways could rot.

Covered in brick dust, tangy blood in her mouth, she burst into an ancient cafeteria. Surrounded by squalling young in a central pool of growth serum squatted a rokkoon that dwarfed the rest. The leaking remains of a previously failed Planter explained the density of mutants. Abosede marked it for Yggdrasil and ran on, knowing WEPAN would fix this.

Thigh-deep in chemicals, chanting a war dirge, Unnulf held off the brood mother's spawn. Through their link Abosede felt his genetics warping. His mood was grim. He did not plan on living.

Six minutes.

Abosede roared. This was her fault. She could not allow it.

She pushed her guilt aside as she felled the first of the charging rokkoons. These were not cuddly, but monstrous with extra limbs and pustulant eyes. She fought to reach Unnulf, hurling a vine from her left arm while her right swung almost mechanically. His own vine caught hers, and she heaved as he leapt free of the pool.

The brood mother screeched in rage, suddenly alone. She trundled at them with surprising speed, muscles rippling and changing as she went. Her DNA had to have been a mess, and they couldn't risk further exposure.

The Gardeners fled.

Four minutes.

Outside, masses of grey-black had gone berserk from their queen's cries. The Gardeners reached Phil only yards ahead of the pursuing horde. He had gotten the Planter into position, moments away from triggering injection rockets.

Two minutes.

"Hit it Phil!" Abosede bellowed, as she and Unnulf sped by, the rokkoon army hot on their heels.

He needed no further coaxing, setting off the explosion and joining their flight. A built-in three-second timer allowed them to put the Planter between them and furry death.

There was a *CRACK!!* as the tree was forced into the earth. Roots erupted outward, shockwaves sending anything nearby tumbling.

"Yggdrasil, are we cleared?" Abosede's lungs heaved.

Affirmative. Planting successful. Congratulations, Gardeners.

The gargantuan TREE flew overhead and tendrils reached down, bringing them back into the embrace of the organic vessel.

As the three of them were detoxed and their esuits autowithered, Abosede did her best to avoid her team's gaze. Phil, ever the empath, brought it up first.

"You OK, Abosede? You're usually doing a victory dance 'bout now."

She yanked a shirt over her treetop-shaped Afro, nearly ripping the cloth.

"I'm getting slow. I've been at this too long, and now I have to choose to be useless, or get one of you killed."

Unnulf stared at her with his oddly large eyes. "Do you suppose being field Gardener is only way to saving the world, team lead?"

They were quiet for a long beat, time cellularly bonded rendering conversation unneeded. What was she afraid of? What was she avoiding?

If she was not a Gardener, the accolades, the respect of her peers disappeared. How would she recognize her value in a world without room for anything extra?

Yet did she not have a wealth of knowledge? Did she not

hold dozens of records? Maybe it was time to help the planet recover by growing more than just trees.

She smiled at Unnulf, at Phil, and shook her head ruefully. They smiled back, knowing her words before she spoke.

"I'll tell WEPAN they have a new trainer tomorrow. Tonight, let's fucking *celebrate!*"

"But no lasting harm." Phil winked.

"And above all else, Gardeners?" Unnulf intoned.

"LEAVE IT BETTER THAN WE FOUND IT!"

ABOUT THE AUTHOR

Liam Burke is an independent author with a penchant for a variety of speculative fiction. His main passion is for juxtaposing biting humour along with the sharp teeth of horror, razor code of cyberpunk, and back alley deals of urban fantasy.

He spends any free time he can either crafting stories with his friends, at the mercy of small plastic polygons on a table, or slaying digital baddies in computerized dimensions. He is a member of the Brooklyn Speculative Fiction Writers group, and possibly several secret societies plotting world domination. Or snack eating. One of those.

Find Liam on the web at http://ssjliam.square.site/

LUNCH FAILURE

Liam Hogan

DOCTOR Jessica Scanlon was half expecting the text message. "Lunch?" it read. Short and sweet, unlike her brother.

On the way down to ground level, she resisted the urge to backtrack, to recheck the setup for the next experimental run. To wait, expectant, for the results. They were sure to disappoint, like all the other recent tests. The team would have to rethink, explore yet another section of the periodic table. Stealing an hour for lunch with her layabout brother wasn't going to change that.

Jess met him by the park entrance, the ribbon of young trees and green lawns that separated the science park from the town proper. A short walk during which she was permitted to talk about her research, before they reached the café and, by mutual consent, the conversation switched to less abstruse topics. Only today, Harry spoke first.

"I got one of those scam aliens yesterday," he said.

"Really? They're *still* doing that?" Jess gave him a sideways look. In the sunshine he looked boyish, carefree. As indeed he was. "I thought they'd have given up by now. You have one unusually cigar-shaped asteroid zipping through the solar system, and suddenly people are getting interstellar cold calls, offering real estate deals on Venus or stock tips from infallible alien supercomputers. I trust you hung up immediately?"

"Well ..."

"Harry! You didn't?" She stopped, midstep.

"I thought I'd play along for a bit, y'know? Just for fun?"

"Idiot!" She would have punched him on the arm if he hadn't been a couple of paces ahead. "You *know* perfectly well what the authorities say. Any snippet of information you give the scammers makes it more likely that you'll be suckered, if not this time, then the next. Even giving them your name—"

"*Sis*, I may not have a fancy doctorate like you, but I'm not a complete moron. I didn't give them my name—"

"*Two* doctorates, actually ..."

"—I gave them yours."

Her feet dragged, and her brother halted as well. A dog walker gave them both a wide berth, tutting as she went.

"You what?! Harry, is this your idea of a joke?"

He had the good grace to look at least a little guilty. "Well, technically they already had your name, I just said I was you, is all."

"Is *all?* You'd best tell me everything they said." Only a younger brother could provoke her this way. "Goddamn it, if this comes back to haunt me I'll have your guts for garters.

With the upcoming departmental review and research funding getting cut ... Since *when* do you do a decent imitation of me?"

"That's just it, I didn't. I said I was you, but I didn't change my voice. That didn't faze them at all."

They set off again, at a slower pace. "Of course not," Jessica scoffed. "They're reading from a script, right down to the 'sorry, there's a delay on the line because we're in orbit around Mars' shtick. Any such delay would average around thirteen minutes, but never shorter than four—they can't even be bothered to lie convincingly. OK Harry, from the top. And don't you *dare* skip anything."

"I don't know why you're getting so het up, Jess. I just played along, for giggles? I *knew* it was aliens as soon as I answered. That distorted voice thing, even before the excuse for the delay. Which is supposedly from Lagrange point 5, whatever that is, apparently a perfect spot to monitor us, with the added benefit that the Cardy-loosky clouds help cloak their presence—"

"Kordylewski?"

"—something like that. In their off-kilter electronic voice, they asked, as polite as you like, if they could speak to Doctor Jessica Scanlon. And I said, in my deepest and most manly voice, i.e. this one, '*Speaking*.'"

Harry's hands fluttered as he eased into the telling of his tale. Jess thought, not for the first time, that he would have made a good court jester.

"And they replied, *yes*, they were speaking, and obviously I was speaking, and could they please speak to Doctor Jessica Scanlon? So I said, since they were playing dumb and I was perfectly willing to play dumber, 'You *are* speaking to Dr. Jessica Scanlon.' And they said how *wonderful* it was to finally get through and they'd been trying for a while, because they wanted to give me—or you, I guess—a solution to a technical issue I was having getting carbon mineralization to lower CO_2 and stop further climate change."

Jessica blinked. *Kordylewski* had been enough of a surprise. "That's awfully close to the truth, Harry."

"Yes, I guess." He shrugged. "But it's not like you keep your research secret, is it? The whole point of a scientific research department is to publish as many papers as possible."

"And save the planet."

"*And* save the planet," he agreed. "That's what they kept going on about: saving the planet. Big spiel about tipping points and stochastic mechanisms and the dangers of alternative geoengineered solutions like reflecting solar clouds and other such nonsense."

Jessica paused for a moment as a jogger ran past, red faced and looking like they were loathing every glorious minute of the unseasonally warm midday run. "I think you mean 'reflective polar clouds?' By spraying salt crystals into them, but yes."

"So not total nonsense, then?"

"Not ... totally." She didn't add that one of the other institute departments was close to a prototype, if they could get the funding.

"Parts of it sounded like that paper you asked me to proofread. Using finely powdered tailings from mines as an integrated building material? Yabbering on about carbonate uptake and how the captured CO_2 would remineralize cracks, making concrete heal itself—"

"That paper hasn't been published yet ..."

"And they said the issues you were having with developing catalysts to increase the absorption rate and engineering suitable nanostructure surfaces would work if you could just ..." Harry trailed off. "Are you OK, sis? You're looking awfully pale."

"Yes, yes, I'm *fine*." Jessica felt like she always did when a car she was travelling in encountered a dip in the road. A fluttering, organs-in-the-wrong-place sensation. "And they had a solution, did they?" she asked, voice and breath tripping each other up.

"Oh yes!" Harry grinned. "They said it was quite simple, actually, and I'd—*you'd*—done most of the hard work already, which they were most impressed by, and it gave them hope in the whole human race however many mistakes they—we— keep making. They said I'd—you'd—probably get there yourself in perhaps as little as thirty years? But Earth didn't have that long, not before the damage was permanent, which was why they were breaking galactic protocol to make this one phone call, and would I—*you!*—kindly never speak of it to anyone and take all the credit for yourself? Because they couldn't sit and watch, not when they had the final piece of the scientific puzzle, the key to turning it from theory to practice, which they were giving to us for free."

"For free?" Jess's voice sounded distant, like it was coming from the next room. She felt the prickle of the sun on her forehead.

"*Yes!*" Harry shook his head, rueful. "I was most disappointed. I was waiting for them to ask for my credit card details to prove I was who I said I was, i.e. you. Or to download an app onto my phone or PC to give them remote access so they could 'send the data.' Or to transfer a fee to unlock an African prince's inheritance."

"*That's* the 419 scam."

"Please, don't remind me. But this lot didn't want anything, which caught me on the hop. Instead, they asked if I was ready to write down what they were about to tell me."

"And ... Harry, were you? *Did* you? Write it down?" Jess's hands clenched and released as she stared at her brother, who stared back, eyebrows raised in amusement.

"Of course not, Jess! It's a *scam*, yes?"

"But ... oh god. Do you remember what they said? Anything at all?"

"No. I'd put the phone down by then."

"You put the phone *down?*"

"I told them we already had one, thank you very much, and hung up." Harry shrugged again, his contented smile that of a grown man declaring "mischief managed." "Hey sis, where are you going? I thought we were doing lunch?"

They'd reached the end of the park, a mere fifty yards of

bright pavement from the café, and the first of the twin church spires that bookended the shimmering high street. But Jessica had turned back the way they'd come. "I can't, Harry. I'm heading back to the lab, and I'm afraid I'm going to be too busy for luxuries such as lunch."

"Too busy? For lunch? *Seriously*, sis? For how long?" Harry called after her.

"Oh, about the next thirty years by all accounts. Perhaps I'll see you then, little brother, if the flood waters or the extreme heat or the invasive species don't get us first."

She glanced over her shoulder to where Harry stood, adrift, and shook her head. He was too far away to hear her, but she said it anyway. "Though even thirty years might be a *lifetime* too soon."

ABOUT THE AUTHOR

Liam Hogan is an award winning short story writer, with stories in *Best of British Science Fiction 2016 & 2019*, and *Best of British Fantasy 2018* (NewCon Press). He's been published by *Analog*, *Daily Science Fiction*, and *Flame Tree Press*, among others. He helps host Liars' League London, volunteers at the creative writing charity Ministry of Stories, and lives and avoids work in London. More details at http://happyendingnotguaranteed.blogspot.co.uk

GRASS STILL GROWS
S. A. McKenzie

MARIANNE pulled the cover over the printing press, and packed the last of the slim volumes in the bags on the floor. The nagging ache in her gut gave a sharp twinge as she bent down. Indigestion, she told herself, but she knew it wasn't. Knowing did no good, anyway. No more chemo, no more wonder drugs. There hadn't been a shipment of any drugs from overseas in years. These days, if you couldn't make it locally, you went without.

She slung a bag over each shoulder and shuffled down the hallway, smiling at Mrs Niroshan, who was tiredly walking back and forth trying to quiet the baby. Behind the closed door of the second bedroom she could hear raised voices. At least the authorities were only sending her one refugee family at a time these days, while they waited for their place on the inland convoys. There had been times when she'd packed up to eighteen people into her three-bedroom house.

Melba greeted Marianne with a loud "Meeeehhhh!" from her stall in the garage. The goat shifted impatiently as Marianne attached the carrier bags to her harness.

"Dude," she said to the goat, as they walked out to the street. "Where's my driverless car?"

Melba knew the answer to that one. "Meee!"

"Goats go where goats want to go. I don't think that counts as driverless!"

She could feel warmth in the wind from the east, bringing a swampy stench with it. *And barely spring yet,* Marianne thought. The mosquitoes would be hatching in the brackish marsh that covered the remains of eastern Christchurch.

She could hear high-pitched giggles as two little boys played in the water-filled pothole that spanned half the street, conducting a naval battle with tiny ships made from flax stems. Dot's granddaughter was hanging out washing in her front yard. As Marianne passed, she sang in a pure high soprano.

Rain still falls and the grass still grows,
Boy sees girl, you know how it goes.

Dot was leaning on the gate watching the kids, and Marianne stopped, yanking at Melba's rope when she tried to sample a roadside patch of cabbages.

"Here," Dot said. "I saved some carrot tops. Did you hear about the latest sea height reading? 10.73 metres! I always wanted a seaside property." She never seemed to tire of that joke.

"Better get that bikini ready," Marianne countered, as she always did, and Dot cackled happily. The truth was there were no more beaches. There was no edge to the ocean any more. It had gulped down half the city, and vomited back a swamp of stinking mud and twisted wreckage.

The last ten years had been a frantic race against the tide to render down buildings and infrastructure to their constituent parts. Everything of possible use, including topsoil and trees, was removed by the Locust Army, to be loaded onto the electric trucks travelling inland, to the new cities. Fairlie, Ranfurly, and even sleepy Naseby had been transformed almost overnight, as the coastal refugees fled to higher ground.

Melba plodded around the corner, a carrot top dangling from her lips. Marianne let the goat pull her along, thinking back over the years. When was it? Was there one particular day? *That day we finally realised things were never going to get better?*

There were those pictures on the news, back when they still got television broadcasts. That shaky video shot with a phone from the last plane to leave Kiribati. The crowds pressing against the chain link fence at the airport. The wave of brown water churned up by the plane's wheels as it moved down the runway. The view of that young woman below, waist deep in the swirling water, holding up her baby over her head, mouth open in a silent O as the plane lifted away. Was it then, when the first nation drowned? Or had they still thought something could be done?

Was it the summer the farmers built pyres of black-and-white carcasses, sending columns of stinking smoke rising up from the plains, after the ships stopped coming and the dairy industry collapsed?

Was it the winter that the flood waters covered south Dunedin, the Hutt Valley, and Greymouth, and never receded?

Or that summer the meteorologists added new colours to their temperature maps, and half of Australia went up in flames? Or the autumn that the first F6 hurricane hit the Caribbean?

Was it the neodengue fever epidemic of 2037, or Black Tuesday when the banks went down for good?

Or that one terrible night when a dirty bomb rendered Sydney uninhabitable. And then likewise Chicago, Los Angeles, Tel Aviv, Manchester, and Marseilles? Or the vicious twelve-day war that turned both North and South Korea into radioactive wastelands, and the last frantic flailing "accidental" missile strikes that took out Japan and half the coastal cities of China?

Marianne shook her head. Maybe it was a different day for everyone who'd lived through the last twenty-five years. She tied Melba to a post outside the old supermarket, now filled with a combination farmer's market and travelling garage sale. A hand-painted sign in the window of the old pharmacy offered "Books, Drugs, and News for Sale. Gossip for Free."

Marianne stuck her head in the door. "Hey, Sam," she

said. "Got a fresh batch for you."

"Marianne, lovely to see you," Sam said, stepping outside to help her carry the bags inside. He laid the slim volumes on the counter, one hand absently scratching the lumpy melanoma on his left ear.

"Diphtheria, symptoms and treatment," he read slowly. "What else have we got here? Goat husbandry, compost toilet construction, Ross River virus, radio operation and repair. Excellent. Riveting reading as always, Marianne."

"At least I achieved my life's ambition," she said, with mock hauteur. "I am a published author, with sales in the hundreds."

"We should have a book-launch party."

"Oh yes, with wine, and those little canapes on silver trays!"

Sam laughed. "I really don't know where I'd get the smoked salmon and crackers." He took out a small notepad and added up some figures.

"With what you brought me today, here's what you have to spend. What can I get for you?"

She was looking out the window at the hills. "Something from the back room. I need 200 mg of morphine, Sam."

"Oh, my dear," he said. "So soon?"

She avoided his eyes. "Not yet. But I'd like to be ready. I don't know how much longer I'll be mobile."

He looked at her for a moment longer, then turned and unlocked the door behind the counter. He returned with a small plastic container.

"Send word when it's time," he said, coming with her to the door. "I'll come around."

"I will," she promised. "I've put some books aside for you."

Outside, Melba had finished the carrot tops and was chewing on her lead rope, a thoughtful expression on her face.

"Come on, you silly goat," Marianne said. "Let's go to the park and you can have grass for lunch."

"Meh," Melba said, agreeably.

Marianne looked up at the green hills as they walked. *Rain still falls and the grass still grows,* she thought. *Maybe I have not had that one particular day yet.*

ABOUT THE AUTHOR

S.A. McKenzie is a New Zealand writer of offbeat and blackly humourous science fiction and fantasy stories featuring time-travelling rabbits, carnivorous unicorns, and man-eating subway trains, because someone has to speak up for these misunderstood creatures. Find them online at www.hedgehogcircus.com and on Twitter: @samckenzie2.

DRUMMING SONG

Ashley Bao

No one really knows where oceans end and where they begin.
Sometimes there is a hulking piece of earth in between, but
there is no barrier between the Pacific and the Indian. The
waters there are blue abysses, no land masses abruptly halting
flow. There are archipelagos stretching from the tip of Asia
to the top of Australia, but they sit within water that has
existed since the formation of the earth.

On one of those archipelago islands, a little girl beats her
drum. Her father made it for her before he left for the bigger
island, searching for work and money to send back home. She
has not seen him in nearly two years, but the teak-wood
instrument reminds the little girl of her father's heartbeat.
When she was a babe, he used to hold her against his chest,
and she would fall asleep to the soft thrum of his heart. Even
now, every time she falls asleep on her cotton mattress in the
room she shares with her siblings, she taps out the rhythm on

the siding of the little drum.

In the morning, her older sisters wake the little girl up before leaving for work. They make and sell jewelry to the tourists who like to admire the mango forests. Every year, the trees dwindle in number as new farms are built to provide food for the foreigners and the mainland.

The little girl is usually left to her own devices. Her sisters have work, and soon she will join them, but the little girl does not dwell on that fact. She simply hugs her drum in close, and beats it on her part of the beach.

Of course, it is not *her* beach, but the tourists stay away from the areas where green algae carpets the water's surface, so it is devoid of other people when the little girl arrives. She sets up her drum and listens to the lull of the tide. The seafoam brushes against her feet as waves crash down upon the sand, washing away the little girl's footprints.

Not so long ago, but long enough ago that the little girl does not remember, there used to be fish in the water. Her father used to hoist her baby body on his shoulders, and he would teach her arithmetic by counting the bright yellow fish languishing underneath the sun. Now, the little girl cannot see those fish so easily. Fertilizer runs down the island from the farms to the coves, the ones the foreigners do not enter.

Bum-budabum-buda-bum-bum

Buzzz

She practices rolls, her palms beating as quickly as hummingbird wings to buzz the sound outwards. For a moment, she forgets about the future she will have to partake in. She forgets about the tourists milling about the island. She even forgets about her father, his kind face that left so many years ago. She remembers the ocean. The water calls to her, licks up to reach her toes. For a moment, the waves move in time with the little girl's drum, stirring up the algae and letting a little bit of sunlight through to the bottom plants.

Eventually, night falls, and her older sisters come to the beach where their little sister plays. Before they take her home, they sit on the sand next to her, listen to the beat of the drum. They remember when the water was clear blue, not obnoxiously green. And the problem has been spreading. Fewer tourists are coming as the ocean no longer remains crystal clear and the fish are no longer as vibrant and numerous.

They don't speak of their worries to their little sister; they would like her to be little forever because to them, it seems as if growing up only makes things worse. Summer monsoons have increased in frequency, the farms have cut down more and more trees, their father sends less money every month. They remember how it used to be, and they cannot figure out a way to reverse the passage of time.

The little girl plays a new song for her sisters. She tells them about the ocean, and the new techniques she learned that day. She tells them about gossip she heard through the sea breeze: there was a way to stop the algae from invading the waters. Seedpods are buried deep in the sand where they will never grow. But they can flourish in the dirt beds at the boundary between shore and mango forest.

Her older sisters exchange a knowing glance. They decide to humour their sister, and together the three of them dig in the sand. The seeds are there, just as she said. They take the small nondescript nuggets of life and bury them in the fertile soil.

"When Father comes back, I want to show him the sea. I want the water to be blue," the little girl proclaims when they finish planting the seeds.

Her older sisters say nothing.

They walk back home, eat dinner, and the day repeats itself until one day, the little girl is not so little anymore. She never forgets her drums or the little patch of shore that was hers alone, but she has to buy food and pay rent, so she spends her days with her sisters selling trinkets to the tourists who remain. Their father stops sending money, and the girl knows she should let go of the promise, focus on tangible needs instead.

Still, there comes a day when business is slow. She finds herself wandering back to her beach. New acacia trees and flowering shrubs line the shoreline. Bright birds roost in their branches. Things have changed since she last played her drums here.

The water at the beach is also different. The green algae has thinned, and the girl can count the tangerine-coloured fish swimming just under the surface. Something in the girl's heart swells as she remembers that day with her sisters. Perhaps the sea breeze was right, and it wasn't just a little girl's futile dreams. She doesn't have to wish the water blue for only her father's sake.

The girl searches in the sand for more seeds, and she spreads them in the soil all along the edge of the island, even venturing out to the beaches where tourists frequent. When her sisters come and ask her what she is doing, she only holds out the seeds.

She tells them to go look at her little strip of beach, how clean it seems now, how full of life. She says, "Though I cannot remember when there were plants in the water other than algae and the fish didn't wash up on shore dead every summer, I know that our future does not have to stay that way. The task is endless: tomorrow I bring my drums to the farmers about using less fertilizer."

Her sisters look at their baby sister: how did she grow up so wise? Once she has finished planting all the seeds, they ask her if she could play the drums for them.

The girl obliges, smiling as she touches the teak-wood instrument. She taps it gently with her fingertips at first. It has been a long time, but she remembers. She plays a song for her sisters, and the ocean calls her again. The waves crash to her rhythm; the tide sweeps against her feet.

On an island in between two oceans, a woman beats a drum, and the water whispers its thanks.

ABOUT THE AUTHOR

Ashley Bao is a Chinese-Canadian-American high school senior. Her poetry and short fiction have appeared in *Reckoning*, *Strange Horizons*, *Cast of Wonders*, and elsewhere. She may sometimes be found looking at cute cats on Twitter @ashleybaozi.

A NEW ONCE UPON A TIME

Greg Beatty

"OKAY everyone!" Mrs. Pratt called. "Time to turn in your drawings of the seasons and line up to go to music class."

Most of the kids cheered at that. A few groaned. All put the finishing touches on their art. Jason added the little frog he put in every drawing. Allison's tongue found its way out of the corner of her mouth, as it always did when she really concentrated. Then they were done too, hurrying to join the rest of the class to go bang xylophones and tink triangles.

After they were gone, Mrs. Pratt went around and gathered the crayons they'd been using. All the blue crayons were pretty worn down, from all the skies. The brown crayons were fairly worn down too, from the tree trunks and leaves. And, as she had come to expect in recent years, the orange, red, and yellow crayons hadn't been touched.

She set the brilliant unused colours in a straight line on the desk in front of her. She took a long slow, breath. Then she methodically smashed the crayons with her stapler, sending a tropical festival of coloured shards exploding to all sides.

"Whoa, Jenn," a voice said. Mrs. Pratt looked up. It was Sharon Williams, who taught the other section of kindergarten. "You know they're just kids, right? Their drawings are supposed to suck."

She was smiling when she said it, to make it clear she was joking, but Jennifer Pratt just shook her head. "That's just it," she said. "They don't suck. It's worse. They're *accurate*. Look!"

She held up a drawing. It was easily recognizable as the school building. Along one side, there were two lines of trees. One line brown and gnarled, both trunk and leaves, like a muddy witch bent with the weight of age and secrets. The other impossibly tall and straight, the trees' dragonfly-wing-like leaves shimmering an electric green in the sun.

"See," Jenn told her colleague. "The little Harris boy captured both kinds of trees: the natural ones, struggling to keep up with the extra CO_2 in the air, and the GMO ones designed for the new atmosphere." Their roots thrived in the presence of plastic fibres in the soil, accelerating their decay.

Without waiting for an answer, she went on. "I know I should be glad for the new trees. They're a big help and a big hope. But darn it, I miss fall. I miss leaves changing colours. And I liked seeing the kids draw them!"

"So, you're destroying the orange crayons because the

leaves don't change colour anymore? What about Halloween?" Sharon asked. She let her voice get small and desperate. "What will they do about the pumpkins?"

Jennifer Pratt laughed, though there was the ghost of a sob audible to both teachers in it. "Oh yes, the Jack and Jill O'Lanterns! Can't leave the kids without any orange for those."

• • •

Though neither woman knew it, across the school, in the fifth-grade science classroom, a similar argument was playing out, this one over textbooks and lesson plans. On the surface, though, it would have seemed completely different: an argument about compliance and regulations.

"So here's the thing," Mr. Ellis explained. "Our funding is tied to student performance on statewide standardized tests."

Mrs. Denton—or "Principal Helen," as she insisted the students call her—smiled a tired smile. "Yes, I am intimately familiar with this requirement, and know just how badly standardized testing measures intelligence, or even academic progress. I could show you studies …"

Mr. Ellis raised a hand. "We're not disagreeing about that, and, as much as tests suck, I'm not complaining about them."

"No?" Principal Helen asked.

"No. I'm asking for something different, something smaller but trickier. I am completely willing to build my curriculum around the mandated tests *or* use the district-mandated materials. However … they don't match up anymore. There was always a gap here or there, but now …"

"Show me," Principal Helen said.

Mr. Ellis did. It didn't take long. The discontinuity was obvious, and so was the cause. One administration had mandated including the most up-to-date science knowledge, to equip students as well as possible to deal with climate change and other rising challenges. Another administration had mandated teaching only sound, traditional knowledge, which they said was to avoid speculative overreach, but which Mr. Ellis maintained was to pacify their base and pretend things weren't changing.

"If it was just their minds they were keeping closed," he said, "I wouldn't care. However, two things are at stake here. First, these are our kids we're talking about. I want them to have the best education I can give them. And second …"

He hesitated, and Principal Helen finished his sentence. "It's our funding at stake, and maybe our jobs."

"I frickin' hate to have to think that way, but … yeah."

The two started brainstorming, torn between several very real and conflicting desires: a desire to teach well, a desire to follow the rules, a desire to keep their jobs, and finally, a desire so deep it was almost wordless.

To have a real answer to the larger questions of change.

Usually when Principal Helen worked out a solution to a multifaceted problem, she liked to use the whiteboard to track ideas, so no one had to depend on their memory and people could literally see connections among ideas. Today, she stood still, with her back to the door, and didn't take any notes. It wasn't until she left, with no answers beyond a promise they'd talk later, that she realized why.

She had been standing with her back to the door because she too was "turning her back" to the problems she was facing, or rather, wasn't facing. And she didn't take any notes because … she didn't want to leave evidence. She trusted that all the parents in her school wanted the best for their children. She didn't trust that they agreed on what that meant, or the best way to go about getting it. Some fired formal charges against school personnel as casually as they reviewed slow service on Yelp. So … no notes, at least not in public.

Shaking her head at what education had become, she left Mr. Ellis's room. As she neared the kindergarten room where they held the after-school programs, she heard a story being told that she'd first heard at her own grandmother's knee.

"And so Cinderella ran from the ball, hurrying to get home before her magic wore off. In her haste, she—"

"Wait, what's haste?" a small but clear voice asked.

"She was hurrying," the storyteller said.

"Like this?" another young voice asked. Suddenly there were scuffling sounds, and what sounded like a herd of light-bodied animals racing around the room.

"Exactly like that," the storyteller eventually said. "And what do you think happened to Cinderella?"

Out in the hall, Principal Helen heard a thump, an "Ow," and then a muttered, "She ran into a desk?"

"No, silly," another voice said. "They didn't have desks at the ball. Wait, did they have desks at the ball?"

Even without seeing the woman's face, Helen could hear

the amused patience in the storyteller's voice. "No. Well, they might have had a table at the side, for refreshments."

"What are freshments?" a third voice asked.

"Refreshments are snacks and drinks. Since it was the king's ball, they might have had more than snacks. Maybe entire roast ducks, and a cook or servant there to carve off slices."

One of the young voices piped up. "Isn't eating roast duck kind of like eating fried chicken?"

"Yes it is," the storyteller replied. "And this was before paper napkins."

"Ewww! What if someone spilled?" A girl's voice rang out. "I'd have to let *a boy* get grease on my gown?"

"Maybe you could freeze it off," another girl said. She followed the suggestion with a "crrruah" sound Helen knew had to be accompanied by a hand gesture aimed at the imaginary offending grease.

"Can she do that?" another boy asked. "I mean, could they do that then? Was magic real then?"

"Of course," one voice said. "That was then. Things were different."

"Of course not," another answered. "Things have always been the same."

"Mrs. Henthorne?" a third voice asked. "They can't both be right."

Ah, Helen thought. *Mary's telling stories today. I should have recognized her voice. This should be good.*

"Do you remember what I said when we first started

story hour?" Mary Henthorne asked.

A pause stretched on, then a girl's voice said, "Was it, 'Harrison, stop pouring that glue on Tarik?'"

Helen laughed out loud at that, but so did Mrs. Henthorne, so none of the kids in the room heard her. When she got control of herself, Mary went on. "Yes, you're right Elise. I believe I used those words exactly. But I meant at the start of the actual story, once all of the glue pouring was taken care of."

Another pause stretched, even longer, interrupted by the sound of small fingers trying to snap. "I got it," a voice said. Then, in a sonorous tone, "Once upon a time, there was …"

"Exactly," Mary agreed. Helen didn't hear what she said next. She pulled her sweater dress tighter around her and slumped against the tile wall. *Once upon a time*. For hundreds of years, those words signalled children that they were entering a strange realm, one where the rules were different. Once upon a time carried children to a world of sudden, causeless change, where wolves talked, puppets came to life, and children got abandoned in forests where witches wanted to eat them.

Once upon a time didn't make the world easy or perfect. Once upon a time didn't mean the story didn't scare the kids, or worse, confuse them.

But once upon a time meant they were in a world where things used to be different from the way they were now. Once upon a time always meant change.

Helen stood up straight and nodded to herself. She'd

forego dinner tonight.

She had an agenda to create for the next teacher training day. There was an interdisciplinary lesson plan on the school's horizon, and maybe some grant money for it. There was that foundation that sent the readers every year, the one committed to making sure fairy tales didn't die out. And there was always money for interdisciplinary projects. Anything that crossed boundaries blossomed money flowers.

Helen knew one thing. She had a tool she could use to help her students and teachers wrestle with institutional, social, and climatic change. Together, they would tell a new once-upon-a-time story, about a world where the leaves changed colours. She didn't have to have all the answers. Kids were used to going back and forth about once upon a time, asking questions and filling in the blanks. Once upon a time made scary change into a shared adventure, and that was a start.

And who knew? Maybe along the way they'd figure out a way for the kids to be heroes, and for the leaves to change colour again.

ABOUT THE AUTHOR

Greg Beatty writes poetry, short stories, children's books, and a range of nonfiction. He's published hundreds of works—everything from poems about stars to essays on cooking disasters.

When he's not writing, he walks with his dog, dabbles in the martial arts, plays with his grandchildren, and teaches college. For more information on Greg's writing, visit https://beattytales.com/

SUMMER ENCROACHING, WINTER YIELDING

Jean-Louis Trudel

THE north wind turned the watery snow into crystal corrugations,
freezing yesterday's footsteps to catch today's unwary feet
an unremembered ramble mashed into icy ridges and rough ledges,
slippery but impossibly hard to batter and kick apart

Such were my father's winters

Cheeks chilled, fingers numb, every breath a cloud,
we fought the cold with love
walked together and resented the season's cruelty,
stealing the grass from us and the sun's warmth,
clasping trees in a killing embrace, and
stiffening the ground it would swaddle and bury in white

Such were my father's winters

Yet, the snow is not so tough,
tomorrow it will pass,
the ice melting away like a bony hand's farewell clutch
(his loosened sinews, his vanishing strength)
winter dies slowly until the sudden spring
    a shock like the collapse of a long-sustained wave function,
    shattered into a single heavy particle
    by a phone call in the night

Such was my father's last winter

Leaving me so little time to mourn—
for spring now runs for the horizon
as soon as it hears winter's slowing tread
a spring ever shorter,
    a flash of green shoots,
    leaves unfolding
    as if panting in haste
for summer's sweltering touch
raining down heat trapped atop a column of tainted air,
feeding the sweat of endless days free of snow and ice

Such will be my winters, shortened and bereft:
his life ended,
yesterday's wind-shaped landscapes crumbled,
and the cold recedes, perhaps forever

ABOUT THE AUTHOR

Jean-Louis Trudel has been writing about climate change since 1988, occasionally as a journalist or teacher but more often as a science fiction author. With over thirty books and more than a hundred short stories to his name, he is also a professor of history at the University of Ottawa, as well as a translator, critic, and convention organizer. Born in Toronto, he now lives in Quebec City and writes (mostly in French) wherever the coffee is good.

CIVILIZATIONS

Tadayoshi Kohno

"LISTEN to me," I think to this human. Ava Martins is her name. "I am here, under your feet. I am in the air all around you. Stop, pause, and listen."

I think these same thoughts to billions and billions of people every day. People seldom listen.

"I need your help," I think to Ava.

Ava listens more than most.

• • •

"Status reports, for each project," I feel the NASA branch leader, Esme Rodríguez, ask those gathered around her.

I feel Ava give a summary of her group's progress on equipment to collect space garbage.

I feel Esme give her acknowledgement.

I feel John give a summary of their group's search for other planets with intelligent life. Their group is scanning, with sophisticated space telescopes, for planets with detectable biosignature gases—gases that are by-products of life. John's group is also scanning for analog and digital radio transmissions, focusing on planets with biosignature gases.

John and their team are completely wrong in their approach. They can find planets with *primitive* life by searching for such gases. But *not* intelligent life.

John doesn't listen to me when I think to them. I think to Ava instead.

"Ava, listen to me," I begin. "I know the other planets in our universe. They are my family. I think to them—the ones who are still living—just like I think to you. Unlike you, *they* know that I am thinking to them, and they think back."

Ava grabs her earthenware coffee mug and sits back in her chair.

"There are no other planets with intelligent life to be found. At least not in our neighbourhood of the galaxy. There were, in the past. But those planets are now long dead. They have been depleted, polluted, and destroyed."

A pit of sadness forms in Ava's belly. Her lips press tightly together and the corners of her mouth turn down.

Ava sits in contemplation as those around her continue to talk. She is no longer paying attention to their conversations. She is listening to me. I think the same message to her, again and again.

Esme calls a close to the meeting. Ava interrupts, saying that she has an idea.

"John," Ava says. "Instead of looking for *living* intelligent life on other planets, maybe we would be more successful searching for *dead* civilizations—civilizations that have destroyed their planets. Maybe we should not be looking for biosignature gases at all. Maybe we should be looking for something else."

Thank you, Ava, for listening to me, the spirit of your Earth. Now, I hope that they listen to you.

• • •

"Are your people starting to listen?" the spirit of one of my sibling planets thinks to me.

"Yes," I think back. "Slowly. There is a reawakening among my people. Many of my people, at least. I am hopeful."

"Good."

"The discovery of dead civilizations on destroyed planets has been motivating to humans. I am sorry, though, that so many of our sibling planets and their intelligent lifeforms have had to die. And I am sorry that it took the discovery of those deaths to convince my people to listen."

"I know."

"I hope their deaths were not in vain. I hope my people can save themselves, me, and all the lifeforms here. And I hope that if you ever develop intelligent life, your lifeforms will take good care of you."

"I have those hopes, too."

ABOUT THE AUTHOR

Tadayoshi Kohno is a professor in the Paul G. Allen School of Computer Science & Engineering at the University of Washington. He volunteers regularly at the Tsubaki Grand Shrine of America, a Shinto shrine north of Seattle. The main character in this story was inspired by Sarutahiko no Ōkami, the Shinto god in charge of Earth and everything within Earth's atmosphere.

ABOUT THE EDITOR

KATRINA Archer is the author of dark fantasy *The Tree of Souls* and YA fantasy *Untalented*, a *Library Journal* Indie Ebook Award Honorable Mention. A former software engineer, she lives on her sailboat in Vancouver, BC, Canada. Katrina has worked in aerospace, video games, and film, and is a freelance copy editor and publisher of climate change site *Little Blue Marble*. She can operate almost any vehicle that can't fly, doesn't believe in life without books or chocolate, and was once owned by a cat more famous in Germany than she is. Connect with her online at www.katrinaarcher.com.

For more great fiction and features about
our changing climate, join us at

LittleBlueMarble.ca

Also available from *Little Blue Marble:*

Little Blue Marble 2020: Greener Futures

Little Blue Marble 2019: Climate in Crisis

*Little Blue Marble 2018: More Stories of Our
Changing Climate*

*Little Blue Marble 2017: Stories of Our
Changing Climate*